"He quit school, I heard," Mrs. Peck said.

Why did she have to mention that!

Aunt Frances was shaking her head. "It does seem a shame, young people quitting school. If they could only realize what they're doing."

"Tony always was a little wild. A nice studious girl like you, Lorrie, could be a very good influence on him."

"I don't think I know him that well." I laughed apologetically.

Aunt Frances didn't look too happy. "Lorrie has other things to do than lure truants back to school. . . ."

## Caprice Romances from Tempo Books

*A CAPRICE ROMANCE*

# Not Your Type
Carol Beach York

TEMPO BOOKS, NEW YORK

NOT YOUR TYPE

A Tempo Book / published by arrangement with
the author

PRINTING HISTORY
Tempo Original / November 1984
Second printing / January 1985

ISBN: 0-441-58891-3

Tempo Books are published by The Berkley Publishing Group,
200 Madison Avenue, New York, New York 10016.
Tempo Books are registered in the United States Patent Office.
PRINTED IN THE UNITED STATES OF AMERICA

## 1

Mr. Ramsey told me it was going to be a snowy winter, the coldest winter in a long time, because he had seen the squirrels burying their nuts early and the robins were already gone and it had rained every Tuesday for four weeks straight.

Mr. Ramsey owned the little grocery store at Willow Lake where Aunt Frances and I lived. He was always making predictions about the weather and other things. Aunt Frances said it was all nonsense, but this time Mr. Ramsey was right. It *was* a very snowy winter and Willow Lake was like a Christmas card picture with snow-covered trees, skaters on the ice, and the dark line of the woods rising beyond the lake houses.

My room faced the lake, and from my window at night I could see the lights of the lodge and the tall black forms of trees and deserted summer houses. Everything was white and silent, and the nearby highway, hidden by the woods,

1

seemed a million miles away. I loved to sit by that window, watching the snow come down and dreaming of Tony Jordan.

Until I was sixteen it was Willow Lake in the summertime.

In the summer, sunlight streamed through the trees, shimmered on the water, created shadows on the grass. From my window I could see the children splashing in the water by Ramseys' pier across the lake. All the houses were open for the summer and the sun glinted on the chrome of cars parked in driveways.

I was seven when Aunt Frances bought the house at Willow Lake, and by the time I was sixteen it seemed we had always come there for the summer and always would. My mother and father had died when I was only a year old; Aunt Frances was my guardian, but she was so good to me that I hardly missed my real parents, whom I didn't even remember. She was an artist, active in her art club during the winter months when we were in Manhattan. In the summer she liked to go sketching in the woods around Willow Lake, and I would go with her, carrying the picnic basket and picking wild flowers. It was my favorite place in the world. I could hardly wait for school to end so we could go to Willow Lake.

My Aunt Adele, whose apartment was near ours in New York City, liked to tell her friends that her sister Frances had "a summer place," but Aunt Adele loved traveling and she couldn't understand why Aunt Frances wanted to go to the same place every summer.

"I love it," Aunt Frances always said. "The lake is so peaceful and beautiful. It's a wonderful change from the city and apartment buildings."

Aunt Adele, with Uncle William and my cousin Barbara, went to places like Florida and the Grand Canyon, and once even to Paris. But every summer they always spent at least a week with us at Willow Lake.

The lake was small, only about half a mile long and a quarter of a mile wide. Circling around it were the Lake Road and the houses; beyond the houses were the woods. At our end of the lake a narrow road led through the woods to the highway. Our house was at the north end of the lake, directly across from the Ramseys' little grocery store and pier at the south end. Most of the activity at the lake took place at the pier and Willow Lodge nearby, so our end of the lake was quieter, more secluded.

The nearest town was Greenwood, five miles away. Whenever Aunt Frances went to get her hair done in a beauty parlor there, I would go to the library and stock up on mysteries and romances to read on rainy days.

Summer at Willow Lake was never long enough. Before we knew it, it was time to close up the house and go back to the city. No more afternoons in the rowboat, hikes through the woods, naps in the backyard hammock on warm lazy days that were not, after all, as endless as they seemed.

Most of the summer families stayed until Labor Day weekend, and by mid-September the lake was deserted except for the Ramseys, weekend guests at the lodge, and a few families that lived at the lake year-round.

Until the summer I was sixteen we had always left the lake by Labor Day weekend along with everyone else. But in the middle of winter, Aunt Frances would remember something she needed that she had left behind at the lake house. We would drive out from New York on a Saturday or Sunday afternoon. How unfamiliar everything seemed then! The lake was frozen over, and there were skaters by Ramseys' pier instead of the shouting children who swam there in the summer. The trees were bare, snow had fallen, and everything that had been warm and green was cold and white. The house itself always seemed rather bleak and forlorn, with dustcovers on the furniture and floors creaking with cold as we walked through.

And yet there was something exciting about the lake in winter, unfamiliar as it was. I wanted to be snowbound, with a fire in the stone fireplace we rarely used in summer. The ice-covered lake looked like a whole new world of adventure. When Aunt Frances had found what she wanted and we came out of the house, I would dart away and run down the snowy bank to try the ice; then run back to the car where Aunt Frances was waiting.

After talking to some people who stayed at Willow Lake year-round, Aunt Frances got an idea: she would fix up our house and we would live at Willow Lake all year long.

Aunt Adele went into a state of shock.

"*Frances,* have you lost your *mind?*" she asked. "Leave New York for that desolate, lonely place—*all winter?*"

"It will be delightful," Aunt Frances replied in her usual pleasant manner. "I can't see why you're so upset."

"You can't see why I'm upset?" Aunt Adele repeated with amazement. "You can't see why I'm upset?"

"No, dear, I can't." Aunt Frances smiled absently.

She seemed to be thinking already about moving arrangements.

"A lonely, isolated lake isn't the place for Lorrie," Aunt Adele said.

"I *love* Willow Lake," I said firmly, but she brushed my words aside with a wave of her hand.

"Where will she go to school, for one thing?" she demanded of Aunt Frances.

"Why, she'll go to the school in Greenwood," Aunt Frances said.

Aunt Adele thought that was a poor plan. "Lorrie should be at Lynden Hall, like Barbara was."

Lynden Hall was the private high school Barbara had attended. I didn't want to go to Lynden Hall. I wanted to live with Aunt Frances at Willow Lake. Aunt Adele seemed so adamant that I was worried for a moment: maybe she would change Aunt Frances's mind and we would keep the New York apartment after all, and I would have to go away to Lynden Hall.

It didn't happen, though. Everything went along perfectly, and by July we had moved out of New York, bag and baggage, and had settled into our house at Willow Lake to stay.

## 2

The lake house was built of chestnut logs and white stone. It was on the side of a little hill, with a sloping lawn on one side and a grove of white birches on the other. Aunt Frances said the birch trees made her think of ballet dancers in graceful poses; to me they looked like the long necks of giraffes stretching up to eat leaves. When I was little, I liked to pat the trees and pretend that they were real live giraffes.

In the summer the big screened front porch was in constant use. It was brightly furnished with a green woven rug and rattan tables and chairs. There were always magazines and books scattered around here and there (cluttered, Aunt Adele would have said) and a mound of fruit in a big wooden bowl on the center table. Aunt Frances and I ate our meals on the porch a lot. It was our favorite spot in the summer. Even when it rained we would eat on the porch—and sometimes that was the most fun of all.

When Aunt Frances decided to live at Willow Lake year-round, a certain amount of ''winterizing'' was necessary, and as the summer progressed we had workmen coming and going. The chestnut logs were heavily caulked, the doors were weather-stripped, storm windows were ordered. The biggest project, however, was the installation of a furnace in the basement.

The summer was an exceptionally hot one. Even the area around Willow Lake was hot, so New York City must have been an oven. Aunt Adele called one night, from the city, to say she was absolutely sick of the heat and would be out to the lake that weekend. Day after day the sun shimmered on the motionless water, and even the noisy children who clustered around the pier at Mr. Ramsey's store seemed lazy and listless in the heat. When Aunt Adele came, with Uncle William and Barbara and a lot of suitcases, Barbara and I walked around the lake to the store. We saw the children running barefoot along the shore, stopping quickly in Ramsey's to buy candy and Popsicles, then running out again, leaving dark wet footprints on the worn old floorboards.

Inside, Mrs. Ramsey stood behind the wooden counter weighing bananas for a woman who had two little children tugging at her skirt.

''Shush, now be good,'' she told the children, and at last they all went out to enjoy their bananas in the shade of the willow trees on the bank of the lake.

Mrs. Ramsey smiled at me, and then gave her attention to Barbara. ''Well, hello there, Barbara. Nice to see you again.''

It never surprised me that Mrs. Ramsey remembered Barbara, even though Barbara was only at the lake a short time each summer. Barbara was the type of girl people noticed and remembered. She was very slender, which was no wonder for she was constantly on a diet. She had long straight blond hair and violet eyes with long lashes. She wasn't as tanned as I was, but I had been at the lake all summer. During her visit she would spend an hour each morning and each afternoon lying in a lawn chair perfecting her tan.

Barbara had graduated from Lynden Hall that spring and was going to start her first year of college in September. On our walk to the store she had told me about the new clothes she had already bought for college, and I knew she would look terrific wearing them. She looked terrific in everything she wore. Even now, in Ramsey's store, she looked like a model on a magazine cover in white shorts and a violet-blue cotton shirt tied at the waist.

"It's always fun to be at the lake," she said chattily to Mrs. Ramsey, and then we began to prowl around, picking out the things Aunt Frances and Aunt Adele had put on the grocery list.

I usually stuck in something extra for myself, like a candy bar or a bag of chips, but when I was with Barbara I was inspired to skip junk food. I wanted to be like Barbara, although it was not likely I would ever have blond hair or violet eyes. I had always envied Barbara's silky hair; mine was light brown and curly. I'd never liked my own hair and couldn't understand why my friends would pay money to have their hair look like mine. Aunt Adele said we all looked like we never combed our hair.

8

When we had gotten all the groceries, Mrs. Ramsey put them in two brown paper bags and we started home, waving to Mr. Ramsey at the far end of the pier as we went past.

"Mr. Ramsey says it's going to be the snowiest winter ever here at the lake," I told Barbara.

"How does he know?"

I laughed. "You know how Mr. Ramsey is. Last week he told me there was going to be fog in the morning because he heard owls hooting in the woods at sundown. And he can tell when it's going to rain by the way the leaves blow."

Mr. Ramsey predicted other things, too, besides weather. Once he told me it was a good year to buy a new car because he had seen a tire rolling down the highway. He said when his right hand itched he was going to get money and when his left hand itched he was going to have to pay out money.

If you saw a crow on Friday it was good luck; but if you saw a crow on Wednesday it was bad luck.

I told Barbara about the different predictions Mr. Ramsey made. I wasn't sure if I believed all of them, but they were fun to listen to.

"Maybe it will be a snowy winter," Barbara said, "but right now it's so hot I can't even imagine snow. When we get back, let's put our suits on and come back for a swim."

When I was alone, I usually liked to swim by the house, but I knew Barbara preferred the pier, so whenever she was visiting we rowed over to the pier to swim. There were boys there, of course, and Barbara always had a flock around her. I wondered if I'd ever be as popular as Barbara. Somehow it didn't seem likely.

When Uncle William came to Willow Lake he liked to sit on the porch and relax. It was quite a change from the busy pace of his business in the city, and he often said, "Adele, we should get a summer place like this." Aunt Adele would smile and say, "Perhaps you're right." But I knew she never seriously considered buying a summer house, and I was pretty sure that once Uncle William got back in the routine of his city life he soon forgot about the slow, relaxing life-style of Willow Lake.

By the time they arrived for their visit that hot summer, the house was just about winterized. Two days after their arrival Aunt Adele was still trying to change Aunt Frances's mind.

"Frances, I'm still not sure you're doing the right thing," she said one afternoon. She and Aunt Frances were sitting in the living room. Uncle William was taking a nap in a porch chair and Barbara, with sunglasses and a magazine, had settled herself on the lawn to get some sun. I was upstairs in my room. I guess my aunts thought I was outside with Barbara because they didn't make any effort to keep their voices low.

I was sitting on my bed, looking out the window as I tried to sew a button on a blouse. I wasn't very good at sewing, but Aunt Frances said I could learn if I just tried. I thought when I was through with the button I would go downstairs and make myself a root beer float as a reward.

My door was open, and I listened; I always listened when Aunt Frances and Aunt Adele talked about me. It was a great way to pick up information.

"Please, Adele, stop worrying about us," Aunt

10

Frances said. "We'll love being here year-round, Lorrie and I. Lorrie's happy to be moving out here."

"I can't imagine why." I could picture Aunt Adele shaking her head at the mystery of that. She would probably be tangling her fingers in her gold chain necklaces and looking distressed. "It will be so lonely. Nothing is going on here in the winter. What will she *do?*"

"She'll go to school," Aunt Frances reminded Aunt Adele. "I don't think she'll lack for things to do with school five days a week and homework on weekends."

Instantly Aunt Adele grasped the subject of school. "School!" she said with a disdainful tone. "If Lorrie's going to school anyplace she should go to Lynden Hall, not some remote small-town school in New Jersey."

"I think Lorrie likes it here better than she would like being at Lynden Hall, really I do." There was a hint of doubt in Aunt Frances's voice, though, and for a moment I forgot that the new furnace was in and the house was all ready for winter, the New York apartment had been given up, our bridges were burned behind us. There was something in the hesitation in Aunt Frances's voice that made me think I would be snatched away from Willow Lake and plumped down at a desk at Lynden Hall. I could almost see the principal now.

"So you are Barbara's little cousin Lorrie. We're delighted to have you with us."

My aunts were still talking. I put down the sewing and tiptoed to the doorway, hoping that Uncle William wouldn't pick that moment to wake up from his nap and come into the house. I didn't want my aunts to change the subject just yet.

But Uncle William went on sleeping, and I went on

11

shamelessly eavesdropping. After all, it was *me* they were talking about. I had a right to listen, didn't I?

"At least I think Lorrie would rather be here," Aunt Frances said, sounding even more uncertain now. "After all, Adele, in two more years she'll be through high school and she'll go away to college. It seems such a short time left to have her with me."

That stopped Aunt Adele. I knew she was sorry she had said anything. Aunt Frances had never married and would never have had any child to care for and love, if it hadn't been for me. And all too soon I would be grown-up and gone away.

"You're probably right," Aunt Adele said at last. Then she added kindly, "I just want to be sure we're doing what's best for Lorrie."

"I think we are," Aunt Frances answered. She sounded more cheerful. "And the school in Greenwood is a very good one."

"I'm sure it is," Aunt Adele said. But she was probably still thinking that Lynden Hall was better.

At any rate, she didn't mention Lynden Hall again. Soon after that, Uncle William came in and Aunt Frances said, "My goodness, four o'clock already, where has the afternoon gone!" She went out to the kitchen to make iced tea, and I heard Uncle William say something about how unusually hot the weather was.

I went back to my room and fiddled with my needle and thread. It had been silly of me to worry, even for a moment. Everything was done, everything moved out of the apartment; even Miss Corbett, who cleaned for Aunt Frances once a week in New York, had been let go. And I had said good-bye to my friends at school.

"I won't be coming back next year," I said, and I told them about Willow Lake. They didn't seem to understand exactly how great it was going to be.

"Oh, Lorrie," one of the girls had said with a sigh, "how can you stand it, leaving the city and everything?"

"Oh, I can stand it," I said. "It's great there in the winter, really." I thought about the ice freezing solid across the lake, and the snowy paths, and the stillness of winter in the woods.

The girls went off down corridors I would never see again, and I thought about my wonderful, beautiful Willow Lake.

## 3

By the end of the Labor Day weekend most of the summer families had closed their houses and left Willow Lake. The lodge was almost empty. Aunt Adele and Uncle William were back in New York, and Barbara was off at college. All the shouting, splashing little children were gone, so the pier was quiet and the Ramseys closed their grocery for the winter. The first falling leaves floated on the water where the children had been swimming, and sometimes I was the only one walking by the shore.

After the bustle of summer, it was as though the stage was cleared for more quiet scenes, and I would look up at the sky and think that soon snow would be falling—the most snow ever, according to Mr. Ramsey.

I began to go to the high school in Greenwood, six miles north of Willow Lake. There were no school buses, but a public bus stopped in front of the Lake Road and dropped me off near the school just before eight-thirty.

I liked riding the bus. Sometimes, especially at first, I watched the scenery; other times I checked over my homework one more time or did some last-minute studying for a test.

The bus went down the main street of Greenwood, where a few stores, a movie theater, and a couple of restaurants still survived the competition of the shopping center north of town. When I got off the bus I had only two blocks to walk to school. Marigolds and cosmos bloomed in the yards of the houses I passed, and there were always a few students clustered around the steps by the main entrance of the school on those warm September days. Then it was October, and the weather turned sharply cooler; the sidewalks were littered with fallen leaves, and the classroom windows were closed.

The school corridors were lined with wooden lockers. In my New York school there were gray metal lockers that changed loudly as everybody scrambled for books between classes. But the Greenwood school was older. The steps between floors were worn in the middle, and in some of the classrooms there were still old-fashioned wooden desks with pencil ledges.

Lockers were assigned the first day of school, and my locker-mate was a girl who was also coming to Greenwood High for the first time. Her name was Darlene, and because we were both new and unfamiliar with things we stuck together and became close friends—though we weren't much alike.

Darlene wore lots of makeup and had frizzy black hair.

She and Barbara would have made a good pair, because Darlene never ate much either, but she did keep a box of chocolate-covered raisins in the locker for emergencies. She taped TV stars' pictures inside our locker door and hung up a mirror so she could check her makeup and comb her hair. With the raisins and the mirror and people like Erik Estrada and Tom Selleck beaming down at us, our locker was a very cheerful place.

Darlene was sixteen, like me, but her figure was much better than mine, and she was not shy around boys, as I was. She was crazy about them and they seemed to be crazy about her, too. There were always a few hanging around our locker between classes chatting with her.

When I confided to her one day that I had never had a boyfriend and that my only dates had been with boys Barbara had fixed me up with, Darlene was amazed. I guess she thought *every*body had boyfriends.

"Is it because your aunt thinks you're too young to date?" she asked suspiciously.

I shook my head. "It's nothing like that at all, really." But Darlene didn't look convinced.

"Honest, Aunt Frances wouldn't mind—at least I don't think she'd mind." Now that I stopped to think about it, I didn't know for sure what Aunt Frances would think if I suddenly started dating boys. The question had never come up.

"Anyway, I just don't seem to have a lot of boys asking me for dates," I said. I tried to sound like I didn't mind. "I guess I'm not the type boys like."

"Of course you are," Darlene insisted. "You're very pretty."

"Do you really think so?" I was delighted; but maybe Darlene was only being polite.

"Sure you are, all that pretty hair—and you have beautiful eyes. You're just sort of shy, but you'll get over that. Don't worry, you'll have lots of boyfriends someday."

This conversation took place one afternoon at a snack shop across the street from the high school called Andy's. It was a combination school supply store and snack shop where the kids gathered after classes. Darlene had discovered it practically her first day at school, and after she started going regularly she invited me to join her.

"Everybody goes there," she said. "It's fun."

I went to Andy's with Darlene one or twice, but since school didn't let out until three o'clock, I barely had time to gulp down a Coke before rushing off to catch the 3:20 bus. I could see this wasn't going to work, and it certainly wasn't much fun, so I decided to ask Aunt Frances if I could stay in Greenwood a little longer after school.

"If I could come on the next bus, the four-twenty, I'd have time to go to Andy's with Darlene."

Aunt Frances wanted to know if Andy's was one of those places where "schoolchildren could get beer and smoke cigarettes."

"Of course not!" I said, laughing. The strongest drink at Andy's was a chocolate shake, and the only thing Aunt Frances really wouldn't have liked was the noise. Between the jukebox and the kids talking back and forth between booths it got pretty loud sometimes.

"Besides," I said, "I probably won't go *every* day. Sometimes I'll have to study in the library after school."

So it was agreed that I would come home on the four-twenty bus. After a week or so I sort of forgot my plan to study in the library sometimes, and I just went every afternoon to Andy's with Darlene.

After the first few weeks of school Darlene began dating a blond, broad-shouldered boy named Steve, and soon he started coming with us to Andy's. He was a senior, which made him seem very exciting.

It was at Andy's, about the middle of October, that I met Tony Jordan.

The weather had been growing cooler. The Woolworth store by the bus stop had Halloween costumes in the windows, and rainy days left sidewalks and school grounds plastered with wet red and orange leaves. Hot chocolate became more popular than chocolate shakes at Andy's. Darlene bought a fake fur jacket to wear with her jeans. She let me try it on and I felt very glamorous. It was time to think about winter jackets and stuff, and Aunt Frances and I drove to the shopping center outside Greenwood and had a grand shopping spree one Saturday.

We both bought new boots. "There's going to be more snow here than we're used to in the city," Aunt Frances reminded me. Didn't I know; hadn't Mr. Ramsey told me.

She didn't want to buy me a fake fur jacket, but I got a brown suede one with a fleece lining. I also got a plaid skirt, two prairie blouses, and new jeans—although Aunt Frances said she thought I had enough jeans already.

The afternoon I met Tony Jordan I had come to Andy's with Darlene and Steve. Darlene and I were talking, and Steve stood up and called to someone who had just come in. We looked over to see whom Steve was calling, and a boy came sort of strolling toward us, hands in his windbreaker pockets, a rather thin boy with dark hair. As he came along toward us Darlene kicked my foot under the booth table and whispered, "Isn't he a fox!"

And he was. His eyes were dark and his dark hair fell across his forehead. He looked better to me than all the TV stars in the pictures in our locker.

"Hey, Tony, where have you been lately?" Steve playfully jabbed the boy with his elbow. "Come on, sit down, sit down." He motioned to the side of the booth where I was sitting across from Darlene, and the dark-haired boy slid in beside me. I moved my books closer to make room for him, and then sat looking down at my French fries and hot chocolate.

Darlene pretended she hadn't noticed the boy until just this moment. "Oh—hi, Tony," she said nonchalantly, as if she had a hundred other much more interesting things on her mind.

Tony answered Darlene with a slight lift of one hand in her direction. Then he turned and looked at me. He seemed amused to see me there, flushing a little and rubbing my greasy fingers on a paper napkin. I wanted to say hello as nonchalantly as Darlene had, but I couldn't say anything at all.

"Who's your friend?" asked Tony, pointing at me.

"Don't you know Lorrie?" Steve said. "Well, now you do: this is Lorrie."

"But Lorrie doesn't know him," Darlene added.

"This is Tony Jordan," Steve said to me. "He used to be a poor student like me—now he's the town playboy."

Darlene giggled.

Tony Jordan ignored Steve. He gave me a sort of

sweeping glance, and then his eyes rested on the stack of books beside me on the seat of the booth. He seemed to find me very amusing. At last he said, "I don't think I've seen you around before."

"Oh . . ." I cleared my throat nervously. "I've been . . . you know, around."

"Lorrie only hangs out in nice places," Steve said teasingly.

Darlene giggled again. "What kind of places do you hang out in, Tony?"

"Listen, kiddo"—Tony looked over at Darlene with a cool, amused smile—"only the best, only the best."

Steve snorted with laughter.

"I'm sure," Darlene answered softly.

She was flirting with him and I glanced over at Steve to see if he realized this. But if he did, he didn't seem to mind. He looked happy and content sitting beside Darlene, and he said, "Lorrie lives out at Willow Lake."

"Is that so?" Tony Jordan looked at me for a moment more, then he got up as abruptly as he had sat down.

"Hey," Steve protested, "you going already?"

"Yeah." Tony drawled out the words. "I got things to do, man."

"Wait a sec—" Steve slid out of the booth and drew Tony aside to talk to him.

As soon as their backs were turned to us, Darlene kicked me again and leaned across the booth, whispering, "Isn't he the handsomest guy you ever saw?"

"He's very romantic looking," I whispered back. "Who is he, a movie star?" I kidded.

"He's a friend of Steve's. I met him in here once

before—you'd already left to get the bus.''

"Does he go to school at Greenwood?''

Darlene shook her head. "Steve told me he quit half-way through his senior year. But he still comes in here once in a while. He would have graduated last year if he hadn't quit.''

"He quit school?'' I'd never known anyone before who'd dropped out of school. "Why did he quit?''

"Who knows?'' Darlene shrugged. "Just didn't like it, I suppose. He doesn't exactly look like a bookworm, does he?''

"No, he doesn't,'' I agreed. But I thought I wouldn't see much of him if he wasn't in school, so I wished he hadn't quit.

"What does he do now?'' I asked. Maybe his family was poor and he'd had to quit school to help support them even though he really loved school. Maybe things would improve at home and he would come back to school. Maybe his locker would be near mine and I would see him every day. Maybe I could be his girlfriend. Maybe—

What was wrong with me? I didn't even know this boy!

"He doesn't do anything much,'' Darlene was saying. "He's got a car and he drives around. Sometimes he works at his brother's garage, part-time.''

The poor family Tony quit school to support vanished. He had quit because he wanted to quit. I was disappointed. But still, maybe he would come back.

And then I noticed the clock.

"Gosh, it's after four,'' I said to Darlene, and began piling books in my arms so carelessly that as I scrambled out of the booth I dropped them all with a huge crash.

21

"What was *that?*" Tony Jordan turned around as the books fell to the floor. I felt my face turn bright red, and I bent down quickly and began to pick up the books to cover my embarrassment. They were scattered everywhere!

I wanted to die—and then Tony Jordan bent down beside me, scooping up all the books quickly and easily. He wasn't laughing at all and I mumbled, "Thank you," as he handed me the books. I was too self-conscious to really look at him, but I could tell he wasn't laughing like the kids in the other booth.

I heard Darlene call, "See you tomorrow," as I hurried away. My heart was pounding as I ran all the way down the street to the bus stop.

The bus wasn't there yet, and I stood by the curb, trying to catch my breath. I was warm from hurrying with such a heavy load of books, and I shifted them in my arms and peered up the street for the bus. Then a car pulled up to the curb in front of the station and someone called, "Want a ride, kiddo?" My heart started to pound again as I recognized the thin handsome face and the dark hair falling across the forehead.

I shook my head and hugged my books to my chest, hoping that Tony couldn't hear my heart thumping. "I'm going to the lake."

"Yeah, I figured that," Tony Jordan said, and he leaned across the seat to open the car door for me.

"Well . . . thanks anyway. . . ." I hesitated, shifting my books again and shading my eyes from the sun with my free hand. Should I get in the car? Should I wait for the bus? What would Aunt Frances say if I rode home with a boy who was practically a stranger?

"Get in, for Pete's sake!"

"It's a long way to the lake." I was hedging for time.

"About six, seven miles, isn't it? A real long way." He laughed.

I cleared my throat and wished I could stop feeling so nervous. "It's nice of you—"

"Will you just get in, for Pete's sake?"

"All right," I said, feeling excited but still nervous. "And thanks a lot."

I got into the car and Tony pulled away from the curb into the heavy afternoon traffic. Gradually I eased my books off my lap to the seat between us and wondered again what Aunt Frances would think about me riding home with a boy I really didn't know.

There was a small diner a block from the bus station, the L&G Cafe. Tony Jordan slowed the car as we went by and honked the horn. I wondered why and looked back as we passed, but the L&G Cafe was lost in the shadows of its faded blue street awning.

A few blocks farther on Tony turned toward the highway, and we were on our way to Willow Lake. I said, "It's warm this afternoon—for October, I mean."

"Yeah, I guess it is," he answered without particular interest.

I wished Darlene were with us. She never ran out of things to say. And she would have thought of something better than the weather to talk about. But I continued bravely: "Everything's so pretty now. It's my second favorite time of year."

"Second?" Tony glanced over at me.

"Winter's really my favorite. I mean because of the snow and all."

He shrugged. "Me, I like summer best."

"Oh, I like summer, too," I said quickly. "I like summer a lot."

He looked at me again and laughed.

He didn't say much after that, except once he whistled in amazement and asked me if I really read all those books I had.

"Well, they're mostly schoolbooks," I answered, "except—"

"I never read books," he interrupted. "I mean, it just seems kind of pointless."

"Oh," I said uncertainly. He seemed to be expecting me to answer him, so I said, "I read books all the time. Not just schoolbooks, but for fun." In New York I had spent hours browsing in bookstores—spent a lot of my money there, too. Once I had started through the children's room at the public library intending to read all the books in alphabetical order. I had been about ten years old then, and I've forgotten where that plan went wrong—it had seemed like such a good idea.

But Tony never read books.

We drove the rest of the way in silence. The highway, a two-lane blacktop, not heavily traveled, wound through woods where the trees were masses of red and golden leaves. Late afternoon sunlight slanted across the road. I wanted to ride on forever and never stop, ride on forever through golden woods with Tony.

All too soon we reached the turnoff road that led down to Willow Lake.

"Why don't you just stop here?" I motioned to a place at the edge of the road that was clear of trees. "I can walk from here."

"How come?" He looked at me curiously.

"The road down to the lake is so narrow and bumpy," I said apologetically. "Aunt Frances says nobody should drive on it if they don't have to."

I thought maybe he'd say that no road was too narrow and bumpy for him, but he put the car in park, settled back, and said, "Okay, kiddo, suit yourself."

Feeling self-conscious, I gathered up my books, opened the door, and got out of the car. He watched, an amused expression on his face, and I was sure he was wondering if I was going to drop my books again.

"Thanks for the ride," I said shyly and started to back away toward the lake road.

He put his hand up to his forehead in a little salute but made no move to leave. I had to turn my back at last as I made my way down the path, and I could feel him watching me trudge through the fallen leaves with my load of books. I felt so self-conscious I could imagine him watching me even when I had taken a bend in the path and knew he couldn't possibly see me any longer.

I went into the house, hugging my books, already falling in love. Aunt Frances looked up from a letter she was writing and gave me a preoccupied smile. "Hello, dear. Is the bus in already?"

"I didn't come on the bus," I answered, setting my books on the table. "I got a ride home from a boy."

I thought she'd have a hundred questions. What boy? How did you meet him? How did he happen to drive you home? But all she said was, "What was that, dear? Oh, a ride home—that's nice," and went back to her letter.

"His name is Tony Jordan."

"Tony Jordan," Aunt Frances repeated, nodding her head. "That's a nice name." Then she forgot about me and went on with her writing.

Aunt Adele would have said, "See, that's just what I mean. Absentminded. The artistic temperament, I suppose."

But I was used to Aunt Frances's ways. I slipped off my sweater and went out to the kitchen to see what Aunt Frances had started for supper. Usually, if she hadn't started anything yet, I suggested things I liked, like chili or spaghetti. On this particular afternoon I forgot about dreaming up my own menu and just sat at the table staring out across Willow Lake—the trees already a mass of gold in the autumn sunlight—thinking about the boy who had driven me home from school. I wondered if he had gotten back to town yet, and if I would ever see him again. Oh, I wanted to see him again!

I knew it was a day I would remember; but I should have heard its warning, as softly whispered as the stir of leaves in a light afternoon breeze. I should have heard the warning, but I saw only the hazy, golden autumn afternoon.

# 4

Mr. Hansen, who mowed grass and did handyman work for Aunt Frances in the summer, agreed to continue in the winter whenever Aunt Frances needed him for odd jobs. And when he heard that Aunt Frances was looking for a woman to come in and clean once a week, he recommended his cousin, Ethel Peck.

"She's a fine worker," he assured Aunt Frances. "Strong as a horse."

"Would she be willing to come in from town?" Aunt Frances asked hopefully. In the short summer months we had always puttered around casually tidying up. But now that the house was our year-round home, Aunt Frances wanted things to be very neat, the way they were in New York.

Mr. Hansen said he'd ask his cousin, and when she said she was interested, Aunt Frances set up a time for Mrs. Peck to come to the house.

The day Tony drove me home from school was a Friday, and the following morning Mrs. Peck came to see about the job. We were still eating breakfast, and Aunt Frances invited Mrs. Peck to have breakfast with us while they discussed the job.

She was a plump, good-natured woman with lots of energy, and she had no objection to making the trip from town. She and Aunt Frances decided that she would come to clean on Fridays, and she never missed a day, even in the worst weather.

Aunt Adele had predicted that we wouldn't find anybody willing to come to the lake to clean house, so Aunt Frances was eager to tell Aunt Adele about Mrs. Peck.

She didn't have to wait long. Aunt Adele came to Willow Lake the Wednesday after Mrs. Peck was hired. It was Aunt Adele's first visit since the summer, her first chance to see how we were getting on. "I would have come sooner," she explained, "but getting Barbara ready for college—what with shopping for clothes and all—I got behind with everything else. Then the end of September was parents' weekend, and of course William and I couldn't miss that. But anyway, here I am now."

She had come alone that Wednesday on the train; Uncle William couldn't leave the city in the middle of the business week. He was going to drive out on Saturday and they would go back to New York together on Sunday.

"William will love this fireplace," Aunt Adele said enthusiastically the first night she was there. The October evenings were quite cold when the sun went down, and

28

Aunt Frances and I had been building fires regularly every night for several weeks. I thought nobody, not even Aunt Adele, could resist Willow Lake sitting in that cheery, high-ceilinged room before a blazing fire. I was right.

"Oh, this is *lovely*," Aunt Adele kept saying. "This is *charming!*" Then she told Aunt Frances, "You must get some of that chemical stuff that makes the flames all different colors—green and blue and yellow. I'll send you some when I get back to New York."

"I can probably get some in Greenwood," Aunt Frances said. Aunt Adele looked as if she doubted that you could get anything in a town as small as Greenwood.

"We'll see," she said. Then she repeated, "William will *love* this fireplace!"

Aunt Frances's plump face looked happy in the firelight. She had wanted to live at Willow Lake for a long time, and now she'd finally made the move. Soon it would snow and winter would really begin. Maybe we'd even be snowbound for a day or two.

"How do you like the school in Greenwood?" Aunt Adele asked, breaking into my thoughts.

"I like it a lot," I said, thinking that since Friday I liked it even better.

Aunt Frances knew Aunt Adele was probably thinking about Lynden Hall, and she seemed to be searching for something to say about Greenwood High School that would please Aunt Adele. "Lorrie has an admirer," she said brightly after a moment. She turned to me. "Isn't that so, Lorrie?"

"An admirer?" Aunt Adele's perfectly plucked eyebrows went up.

"That's right," Aunt Frances said. "He drove her

home from school the other day.''

Before I could say that Tony was hardly an admirer—he seemed to be constantly laughing at me—Aunt Adele began questioning me.

''And who is this young man?'' Her tone was light, but I knew she was more serious than she sounded.

''He only drove me home once—''

''But that's very nice. A boy you met at school?''

''Not exactly.''

How could I explain? Aunt Adele was waiting.

''He's a friend of some kids I know at school. I met him in the snack shop after school.''

''I see.'' Aunt Adele nodded and waited for me to go on.

I knew I was trapped. ''He quit school.''

Aunt Adele's interest faded into an expression of disapproval, and Aunt Frances looked confused. ''Oh. I don't think you mentioned that to me, did you?'' She glanced at Aunt Adele apologetically.

''Quit school?'' Aunt Adele studied my face. ''How old is he?''

''About eighteen, I guess. He's—'' I'd wanted to say he was very handsome, but I knew that Tony's good looks wouldn't make up for his quitting school.

''He's what?'' Aunt Adele wanted to know.

''He's very nice.''

''Why on earth did he quit school?''

''I don't think he liked it.''

''Well, honestly, Lorrie, that's hardly a reason,'' Aunt Adele said, looking at me as if she thought I was being fresh.

I could sense my aunts' disappointment that the first boy to show some interest in me had to be a high school dropout.

"What does he do, dear?" Aunt Frances asked, after clearing her throat and glancing at Aunt Adele apologetically again.

It was silly, but suddenly I wished I could say something redeeming about the dark-haired, handsome boy. Even though the two of us didn't seem to have much in common, he seemed like such a friendly person. He'd given me a ride home even when I'd told him that I lived way out by the lake. But I knew that wouldn't impress my aunt, either.

I said, "He works at his brother's garage."

Aunt Adele leaned back into her chair; the discussion was over as far as she was concerned. I could practically hear her thinking: A *garage* . . . well, *really!*

Aunt Frances broke the strained silence that followed with a bit of news about one of the art galleries in New York. She kept in touch with her art club and intended to exhibit in a New York gallery in the spring.

I knew they were both disappointed—and disapproving—about Tony; Aunt Frances was surely wishing she'd never mentioned him in the first place. When I went up to my room at last, I lay across my bed looking out at the dark shadows of trees rising around Willow Lake, and I was curiously reminded of a time many years before when I had found a black puppy on the front steps of our apartment building. There it was, looking for a home. Aunt Frances had thought the puppy was adorable, and only after we had been playing with it for half an hour or so did she suddenly remember that dogs were not allowed in our building.

I was about eight then, and I cried and cried, pleading that it was only a tiny little puppy; and into this scene of tears Aunt Adele had entered, straight from her hairdresser, fresh and beautiful and dripping jewels.

"But, Lorrie, sweetheart!" she crooned, lifting me up into her arms. "Mustn't *cry!*" Then I heard her whispering to Aunt Frances over my head: "It's just a stage— Barbara went through the same thing—the 'pet' stage."

Then she tilted my chin up and smiled at me. "We can give the puppy to Mr. Samuels; he'll know someone who can give it a home." Mr. Samuels was the maintenance man in our building; both my aunts always thought maintenance men could solve almost any problem.

"And then," Aunt Adele continued cheerfully, "I'll tell you what, Lorrie: On Saturday Barbara and some of her friends are going to the circus and you're invited to come, too. Now, won't that be fun?"

"We could hide it," I wailed.

Aunt Frances looked distressed, but Aunt Adele only laughed gaily. "Naughty, naughty," she teased me, drying my tears with a tissue she had taken out of her purse.

"No, that wouldn't be right at all," Aunt Frances said. She twisted her fingers and stared at the puppy regretfully.

When Aunt Adele had gone I cried some more, and then I persuaded Aunt Frances to let me keep the puppy just one night, just until morning. And I made the puppy a bed with a blanket in an empty hatbox, sure in my heart that when morning came I could beg for one more day, and then one more day after that, and one more, until he would be mine forever. I named the puppy Blackie and put it to sleep in the hatbox right next to my bed.

Unfortunately it turned out to be a night when one of Aunt Frances's friends from the apartment below came up for a chat. Just as I was falling asleep the puppy began whining; I got out of bed, took it in my arms, and huddled in a corner behind my dresser. Any moment I thought Aunt Frances's friend would say, "I hear a puppy! Puppies are not allowed in this building!"

It was cold and uncomfortable crouching behind the dresser, and the puppy didn't want to be held. He wriggled and whimpered, and I thought the lady would never go—but I still wanted to keep the puppy, whatever the problems were.

In the morning the puppy was already gone when I woke up. Aunt Frances had given it to Mr. Samuels, so my plan to beg for one more day was over before it began.

That Saturday afternoon Aunt Adele turned up, as she'd promised, and took me off to the circus with Barbara and three of her girlfriends.

But even in the midst of the noise and band music and bright lights of the circus, watching the balloons and clowns and daring trapeze performers, I didn't forget the little puppy. I would rather have had the puppy back again than a hundred trips to the circus.

I wished Aunt Adele had never known about the puppy. I was sure Aunt Frances and I could have worked out *something*.

And now I wished Aunt Frances hadn't told Aunt Adele about Tony. Although I hardly knew him I wanted to protect him from her disapproval.

He'd only driven me home once; maybe I would never see him again. But somehow I wished Aunt Adele didn't know about him.

# 5

After the day Tony drove me home from school, I didn't see him for two weeks. I still went to Andy's with Darlene and Steve after school, but Tony never showed up.

"I wonder where your friend Tony is these days?" Darlene asked Steve once.

Steve just shrugged. "Who knows about Tony? Probably busy at his brother's."

"You mean the garage?" I asked.

"Yeah." Steve nodded. "Sometimes it gets real busy there and I don't see Tony for weeks."

Why couldn't Tony just be in school like everybody else? I thought impatiently. Darlene giggled and Steve tousled her hair and said, "Hey, what's all this interest in Tony?"

"Don't be silly," Darlene said, looking particularly

pretty in a new cowl-neck sweater and matching blue eye shadow. I wanted to go on talking about Tony Jordan, but Darlene began to tell me how her father was threatening to cut her allowance again, which in Darlene's opinion would mean the end of the world.

Darlene always had problems at home. Her father didn't understand how she *needed* certain important things, like clothes and makeup; her little brother was always getting into her things; her mother catered to everyone except Darlene; and her sister Anna May was the worst of all. "She makes all this money," Darlene confided, "and she's so stingy she won't let me wear any of her clothes." Anna May worked at the Greenwood phone company, where she had gotten a job when the family moved to town during the summer. Before that she had worked in an insurance office. She was twenty-two, and she had been working and making money and buying lots of beautiful clothes for four years, but she refused to share anything with her own sister.

I had always thought it would be fun to have a sister, but Darlene said it wasn't all that much fun. "Just wait until I get out of school," she promised. "I'll make lots of money and spend it all on clothes!" Then she asked, "What are you going to do, Lorrie? I suppose you'll go on to college?"

"Yes, I suppose so," I replied.

Darlene considered this. "Well," she said, "you should, you're so smart and everything."

"Don't you want to go to college?" I asked.

"Me? No, not especially. I'd rather get a job and have some fun."

It made me think of the paths that stretched out ahead of

us. There were so many ways to go, so many decisions to make. Smiling to myself, I couldn't help thinking of Aunt Adele, who knew which path was best not only for herself but for everybody else as well. Life posed no difficult problems for Aunt Adele; she always knew just what should be done.

Although Darlene and I were headed toward two very different ways of life, our friendship seemed eternal during those days at Greenwood High. Besides going to Andy's and sharing a locker, we had two classes together: English and gym.

I didn't have any special friends in any of my other classes, though I tried to be friendly with a girl who sat across the aisle in my Spanish class. We were usually the first to arrive in the classroom.

"*Habla usted español?*" I said one day, trying to start a conversation. "*Cómo está usted?*"

Darlene would have laughed and said, "*No comprendo,*" or something silly like that, but this girl stared at me as though I had two heads.

The next day I tried again, this time in English.

"I like your blouse."

"Oh, thanks," the girl said. Then she began to talk to another girl who sat across the aisle from her on the other side. I leaned forward and tried to get involved in this conversation, as the classroom slowly filled with students. But they ignored me and talked as if they'd known each other for years—which they probably had.

Well, I had Darlene—and of course I was always hoping to see Tony again at Andy's. Two weeks later, I did see him again, but not at Andy's. It was at the bus stop. He pulled up to the curb just as he had done before and called to me as though it had been only yesterday and not two weeks ago that he'd driven me home.

"Hi," I said shyly, walking over to the car.

"Hi, kiddo." He looked at me with that same lazy amusement. "Still got the books, I see."

I laughed nervously. "I've still got the books."

I thought of all the afternoons I had secretly looked for him at Andy's. Now here he was—as handsome as I remembered, with his dark eyes and teasing smile. I looked away, pretending to watch for the bus.

"Come on," he said, "get in. I'll take you home."

"Oh, you don't have to do that." I didn't want to seem too eager. "The bus is coming."

The bus was not only coming but had already begun to honk at Tony's car, which was in the bus zone.

"Come on—before I get run down by that bus." Tony opened the door and I got in beside him. My books tumbled on the seat between us, and the bus honked again as Tony jammed down on the accelerator and we shot away from the curb with a wild squeal of rubber on pavement.

"I hope I'm not going to have to go through this every time," he said to me.

"Go through what?" I could feel my face getting flushed.

"All this arguing."

I laughed nervously again, wondering how, after sixteen years of living, I couldn't think of anything to do except laugh mindlessly and stare down at my shoes.

As we passed the L&G Cafe Tony honked, as he had done before.

"Why did you honk?" I asked. Good! Something to talk about.

But he only shrugged and acted like my question was just a joke. So much for conversation.

We were soon out of town, on the road that wound through the woods, and he asked, "So how do you like living at the lake?"

"I love it."

"It's nice there," he agreed. After a moment he added, "I go to the lake to skate sometimes. How come I've never seen you?"

"This is our first winter," I said. "We've always just come for the summer."

"I've been there to swim in the summer, but I don't remember seeing you."

"I swim by our house more than at the pier," I said. I was thinking that even if he had seen me, I wasn't the kind of girl he would have remembered.

"How come your folks decided to live there?" he asked.

"Well," I explained, "I don't have folks, the way you mean. My mother and father died in a car accident when I was little and I live with my aunt."

He looked over at me with surprise and sympathy.

"It's not as sad as it sounds," I said. "I didn't ever really know my parents. Aunt Frances is just wonderful. And there was my grandmother, too, when I was little, but she died when I was about six."

After a moment he said, "So what does your aunt do for a living?"

"She's a painter, but she doesn't have a regular job the

way most people do.'' It was crazy to be telling all this to a boy I hardly knew, but I went on. ''There were the three sisters: my mother, my Aunt Frances, and my Aunt Adele. Since my Aunt Frances was the only one who wasn't married, my grandfather left her most of his money so that she could continue her painting without worrying about money. And of course she makes money painting, too.''

''Sounds like a nice setup,'' he said.

''I guess it is. I never really thought of it all that much.'' Then, after we had driven a little farther in silence, I asked, ''What do you do, Tony?''

''Um . . . different things,'' he answered vaguely.

''Darlene said you worked at your brother's garage sometimes.''

He looked over at me, his eyebrows lifted in mock surprise.

''Is that what Darlene says? And who's this Darlene?''

''You know. *Darlene*. Steve's girlfriend.''

''Oh, *that* Darlene.'' He was laughing at me, I knew, but it was nice, as if he liked me and liked to tease me.

''What else do you do? I mean, besides working at the garage?''

''Sometimes I work with my old man.''

''What does he do?''

''He's a housepainter.''

''Oh,'' I said. ''Then we both have painters in our family, don't we?''

''Yeah, I guess we do.''

When we got to the path that led down to the Lake Road, Tony pulled to the side of the road as he had done before. But this time he turned off the ignition, and when I reached for the door handle he caught my arm.

"What's your hurry?"

I was startled that he had touched me, and when I didn't answer his question he asked again, "What's your hurry?"

"No hurry," I said. What was going to happen now?

He let go of my arm and looked around at the woods. "It's nice here," he said. "I always thought I'd like to live around here myself. Someday I think I'll build a house by the lake."

"Yes, it's nice," I murmured. It didn't seem the time to suggest that people who built houses usually worked hard at something first, to make the money.

"You know where I think I'll build it?" he continued. "On that lot about the middle of this side of the lake, the one near the lodge. You know the one I mean?"

I nodded. He had a thoughtful expression on his face, as if he could already see his house built there, on the biggest lot of land, on the highest hill.

Aunt Frances would be wondering where I was. The afternoons were getting shorter, and already the sun was gone from the wooded area around us. In a few more weeks it would be almost dark by this time of day.

I wanted to stay with Tony, and I sat there as long as I dared, while the sun sank lower and lower.

"I've got to go," I said at last, gathering up my books.

"Okay, kiddo." He looked at his watch, and he was already starting the car as I got out. He didn't stay to watch me, as he had before. He drove away while I was standing by the side of the road. It was my turn to watch him. He

made a U-turn and disappeared back toward town, and I
wondered when I would see him again. There was a whole
long weekend before I would be back in Greenwood
waiting at the bus station after school . . . and maybe he
wouldn't even be there then.

When I got to the house Mrs. Peck was just finishing for
the day. She was untying her apron as she saw me come up
on the porch, and she waved through the window. Aunt
Frances was coming out of her studio, a folio of sketches
open in her hands. She was riffling through the sketches
hastily and muttering to herself because she couldn't find
what she wanted.

"Hello, dear," she greeted me absently, looking
pleased to find me there.

"I got another ride home from that boy," I blurted out.

"What boy? Oh, you mean *that* boy—what was his
name—Tony something, or was it Tommy . . . ?"

"Tony," I said. "Tony Jordan."

"Tony Jordan?" Mrs. Peck jumped into the conversation with a cheery smile. "I know his mother."

"Do you?" Aunt Frances looked vaguely satisfied, as
if Mrs. Peck had said something helpful.

"My goodness, yes," Mrs. Peck said. "I've known the
whole Jordan family for years and years. I went to school
with Tony's mother and father."

I was afraid the mention of school would remind Aunt
Frances that Tony didn't go to school, but she seemed to
have forgotten that we'd ever talked about Tony before
today.

"Tony's a good boy," Mrs. Peck continued. She
folded her apron as she talked. "He quit school, I heard.

42

That's too bad.'' She shook her head.

Why did she have to mention that!

Aunt Frances was shaking her head, too. ''It does seem such a shame, young people quitting school. If they could only realize what they're doing.''

''That's what I always say,'' Mrs. Peck agreed solemnly. Then she added, ''Tony always was a little wild.''

Aunt Frances looked taken aback. I suppose she was wondering just how wild Tony was.

''He doesn't seem wild to me,'' I said quickly.

To me he was a boy kind enough to help pick up my books when everyone else was laughing; a boy who sat looking through the woods toward an imaginary dreamhouse he would build someday beside a lake.

''Oh, not so awfully wild,'' Mrs. Peck admitted. ''Just a little.'' Then she smiled at me approvingly. ''A nice studious girl like you could be a very good influence on Tony. Who knows,'' she said thoughtfully, ''you might get him interested in going back to school again.''

''I don't think I know him that well.'' I laughed apologetically. ''But it would be nice if he went back.'' (It would be *terrific*.)

Aunt Frances didn't look very happy. ''Lorrie has other things to do than lure truants back to school,'' she reproached Mrs. Peck gently; and Mrs. Peck agreed at once that that was true. She gave me a wink, letting me know that she still thought my luring Tony back to school was a good idea, and then she put on her coat, got into her Volkswagen, and went home.

When I went upstairs to change into leg-warmers and an oversized flannel shirt—my favorite lounge-around-the-

house clothes—I stood for a few minutes looking out of
the window that faced the birch grove at the side of the
house. I wished that Mrs. Peck were right, that I could be
such a good influence on Tony Jordan that he would give
up his going-nowhere life and come back to school; but it
didn't really seem likely. I couldn't even figure out why
he liked me enough to drive me home from school. He was
so handsome I knew he must know lots of girls!

He was the first boy who had ever really paid any
attention to me, and it was wonderful that he was so
handsome, and it was terrible that he was so different from
me. "I never read books," he had said. I knew if he
looked out of my window at the birch grove, he would
only see a birch grove and not giraffes, as I did, or Aunt
Frances's ballet dancers.

# 6

On Monday I told Darlene that Tony had driven me home again, and she rolled her eyes dramatically. "Lucky you!" she said. We were at our locker, and Darlene had been admiring her hair in the mirror. "I wish he'd drive *me* home someday."

"But you only live a few blocks from school," I reminded her.

"That's not the point." She giggled, admired her hair one last time, and closed the locker door. Then, more seriously, she added, "I don't think either of us is going to get very far with him. He has a girlfriend."

A boy passing in the hall called to Darlene and she turned, waving her fingers and calling, "Hi, yourself."

"He has?" I asked dumbly.

"Has what?" Darlene's attention came back to me.

"Oh, you mean Tony. Yup"—she sighed regretfully—
"he has a girlfriend, I'm sorry to say."

"Who?"

"A waitress at that lunchroom down the block from
where you catch the bus."

"The L&G Cafe?"

"That's the place."

"How do you know about her?"

"Steve pointed her out to me one time. A redhead."

"Oh." I suddenly felt sort of lost and lonely. "Is she
real cute?"

"She's cute enough, I suppose," Darlene said. Then
her face lit up. "Hey, Lorrie," she said. "Steve's absent
today. Why don't we go to the L&G instead of Andy's
after school, and I'll show you Tony's girlfriend."

"Really?"

"Sure."

I thought that was a very exciting idea.

It was almost time for the bell to ring, and we hurried
along the hallway, parting at the head of the stairs by my
Spanish classroom.

"See you later," Darlene called back as she ran down
the stairs to her class. "Later" would be our gym class
together just before lunch period.

I wanted the day to speed up to three o'clock. I couldn't
*wait* to see what Tony's girlfriend looked like. I was
curious to see what kind of girl he dated; I was a little sad
that he wasn't interested in me. I rushed into my seat in
Spanish class only a moment before the bell rang. I was
always there early, and the girl across the aisle gave me a
look of surprise. I guess she thought I would never have

anything else to do that could make me late for class.

I thought the day would never end, but it was finally time to meet Darlene at our locker after the last period. We hurried to the L&G Cafe and, like two conspirators, slid into a booth opposite the long yellow-and-chrome counter.

"There she is," Darlene whispered as soon as we had sat down. I peeked around the side of the booth. Behind the counter, which was almost deserted at that hour of the day, a waitress with a ruffled white apron and beautiful long red hair glanced over at us and took a menu from the counter. She came toward our booth, and I ducked back into place and pretended to look out of the window at the theater marquee across the street.

"We both want milk shakes," Darlene said, forgetting her diet for the moment, and as the waitress went back to the counter we both watched her slyly. She made the milk shakes herself, chatting to a man sitting alone at the end of the counter. She looked at least as old as Tony, maybe older; certainly she was a lot older than Darlene and I were. And she *was* pretty. Besides her gorgeous hair, she had a great figure and pretty blue eyes.

When the waitress came back with our milk shakes, Darlene said boldly, "I don't suppose you remember me?" The red-haired girl looked at Darlene blankly, and Darlene continued, "I was in here one night a couple of weeks ago with Steve, Tony's friend."

"Oh, yeah, sure," she said with a blank look. I'm sure she saw a lot of people in the cafe and couldn't remember them all. "Nice to see you again," she said, and went off to wait on a woman who had just come in. Every once in a while she would say something to the man who was still sitting at the counter, and he would laugh at whatever it was she said.

"Look at her!" Darlene whispered. "What a flirt! I guess Tony likes that." There was a touch of envy in her voice. "Steve told me Tony comes in here to pick her up after work at night."

"Every night?" I asked. I was overcome with sadness at this thought.

"I don't know if he comes *every* night." Darlene studied the waitress again. "I'll bet she's got some other guys, too. Tony's probably not her only boyfriend. Look at her flirt with that man, Lorrie. Honestly!" Darlene wrinkled her nose with disgust, as if she herself would never think of flirting.

We drank our milk shakes slowly, so we could stay longer. No one else came in for a while, and the waitress stood talking to the man.

"What's her name?" I whispered at last.

"Oh"—Darlene wrinkled her nose again—"who knows." Suddenly she clapped her hand over her mouth for an instant, then she said, "Lorrie, wouldn't it be terrible if Tony came in now, right now, and saw us sitting here!"

I'd never thought of that. I knew I had to get out of there—fast. "Come on, let's go," I whispered. Then I suddenly wondered what time it was. According to the clock over the counter it was 4:25. I had missed my bus. It had probably gone right by outside the cafe while Darlene and I had been sitting there peeking at the waitress behind the counter.

48

"You missed your bus." Darlene followed my glance up to the clock. "What'll you do?"

"I'll have to call Aunt Frances." It was the only thing I could think of. The next bus wasn't due for another hour. I'd have to let her know I'd be late or see if she wanted to come and get me.

"There's a phone." Darlene pointed over to a corner of the lunchroom, and as I went past the counter to the phone the waitress was still talking to the man and he was still laughing at everything she said. She must be quite humorous, I thought wistfully. Besides being pretty and having pierced ears and gorgeous legs.

I tried to make my phone call as quickly as I could; after what Darlene had said about Tony coming in I wanted to get out of the place right away. Otherwise I was sure it would happen: he would come in.

"Aunt Frances said she'd come and get me," I told Darlene when I got back to the booth. I didn't bother to sit down again, just picked up my books. "Now let's get out of here. If you want to wait, we'll drive you home."

"Sounds great." Darlene picked up her things and followed after me, and at last we were safely outside the L&G Cafe without being discovered by Tony. What a relief!

It took Aunt Frances about fifteen minutes to drive from the lake, and Darlene and I wandered across the street and looked at the pictures outside the theater. There was a secondhand store next door to the theater, and we browsed around in there for a few minutes. Darlene bought a scarf for twenty-five cents. I had never been in a secondhand store before, and I thought it was very interesting. It had a dusty, old-fashioned look, as if it didn't belong in the twentieth century. There was a table at the back covered with secondhand books. They were rather worn, but I bought a mystery novel for twenty cents.

It had been an exciting afternoon—seeing Tony's girlfriend without getting caught and discovering the secondhand store. But I knew the thing I would remember most about the afternoon was the sad, lonely feeling I had when I thought of Tony and the waitress.

When Aunt Frances came we drove down Cedar Street to take Darlene home. Her house was a small brown frame house with a side porch and a bicycle parked by the steps—her little brother's, I supposed. It looked like a comfortable, cozy house. Lights were already shining through the downstairs windows. Darlene's mother was probably cooking supper, and soon Anna May would be home from the phone company office. Darlene waved back to us as she ran up the walk to the house and nearly tripped over the bicycle.

As Aunt Frances and I headed out toward the lake it was already dusky and cold. I sat with my books stacked on my lap, fiddling with the clasp on my purse and staring out of the window at the darkening woods. I knew now why Tony honked when he drove by the L&G: it was either to tease his girlfriend, who would look out as he went by and see him with another girl—maybe this was why he offered to drive me home—or it was a secret signal between them. I didn't like either reason.

# 7

About this time I was reading *Les Misérables* for my lit. class, and I'm sure I will always think of October's last bright days and the beginning of winter whenever I think of *Les Misérables*. It was a big book and took me a long time to finish; the weeks of autumn became the weeks of early winter, but my mind was far away in the France of another century.

The day after Darlene and I had gone to the L&G Cafe, while I was waiting at the corner for the bus, Tony drove up to the curb.

"Hey, look," he said firmly, "why don't you just get in and skip all the arguing this time?"

"All right," I said, trying to look sophisticated, like the red-headed waitress at the cafe, as I got into the car.

Tony's next words, however, startled me so that I forgot to be sophisticated.

"So where were you yesterday?"

"Where was I?" I echoed stupidly. "Oh—I missed the bus." I could hardly believe that while Darlene and I sat whispering about his girlfriend, Tony had been looking for me at the bus stop. "Were you going to drive me home?"

"I thought about it," he answered carelessly. "I get to feeling sorry for that poor old bus. I don't know if it's strong enough for you and all those books. What's *this* one?" he asked, pointing to *Les Misérables*. "It's huge!"

"It means 'the unfortunate ones,' " I explained.

"Sounds cheery," he said.

"I could have had *Crime and Punishment*. We had our choice."

"Some choice!"

"It's very exciting. . . ." I began. I wanted to tell him about Jean Valjean escaping from prison and about Fantine and Cosette and all their problems, but the look on his face made me stop. He really didn't care about it. I knew he didn't care, and my wishing he were different wouldn't change a thing.

We were passing the L&G Cafe, but Tony was still remarking on all my books and I was more aware of the L&G than he was. I wondered what his girlfriend would think if she saw him whizzing by without remembering to honk the horn.

"So you missed the bus?"

I nodded vaguely and tried to think of something to say to change the subject before he asked any more questions.

"How come you missed the bus?"

"Ohhh . . ." I dragged out the word to kill time while I thought of what to say. "I was with Darlene. We just got talking, you know."

Tony laughed. "You girls. Talk, talk, talk. My sister's just like you. She and her girlfriends. Man, they never stop."

"I didn't know you had a sister." I seized the chance to change the subject. "What's her name?"

"Peggy. She's just a kid, though, she's still in grade school. I guess she'll graduate this year."

I had a flash of memory of myself as an eighth-grader, unsure of myself, worried about starting high school, longing to be like my cousin Barbara. Clothes never fit right, boys liked other girls. I was sure, though, that Peggy's life was very different from mine.

I envied the waitress at the L&G Cafe; now I also envied Peggy Jordan, an eighth-grade girl I had never even seen. Tony was so much more a part of their lives than he was of mine. I watched the road ahead, unwinding before us in the dull winter light. And I wished I could be part of Tony's life.

When he let me out of the car at the lake he said, "Maybe I'll see you tomorrow, kiddo." And for the rest of that week and all of the next, he came by the bus station every afternoon at 4:15. I would always try to look casual when he came by so he wouldn't think that I was looking for him. Once, when I was afraid he wasn't coming, I thought I couldn't bear to get on the bus and go home alone. My hair had turned out perfectly that day, and I had fixed all my makeup just right before I left the booth at

Andy's where Darlene and Steve were still talking. I wanted Tony to see me today. And he wasn't there! Then I saw him coming along, just ahead of the bus, and everything was okay again.

Sometimes, as we drove along, I could hardly think of two words to say; other times I couldn't stop talking and I heard myself chattering on about things that happened at school, things that weren't even very important, anything just to keep talking. Then, when I'd pause to catch my breath, Tony would look over at me with his lazy smile, amused that I was talking so much.

I always told Aunt Frances whenever Tony drove me home. I knew she was pleased that I had a sort of boy-friend, but she was still doubtful as to whether he was the right one. I wished I could walk in from school some afternoon and say, "I got a ride home with Tony Jordan—and by the way, he's back in school." I was sure that would have made everything all right.

I could tell Aunt Frances was not sure what to do or what to say about Tony; finally one afternoon she said, "I suppose this boy will be wanting to take you out on a date one of these days."

"I don't think so," I said, trying to sound as if I weren't hoping for just that. "He just drives me home to be nice. He has a girlfriend."

"He has?" Aunt Frances looked surprised. "Well, I don't understand, Lorrie—" We were interrupted by the phone ringing, and I escaped up to my room as Aunt Frances answered the phone. I was sure what I had told her about Tony not asking for a date was true, and I didn't want to think about it.

And yet the very next day he almost did.

There was a steep hill about a quarter of a mile from Willow Lake. One side was clear of trees, and one afternoon as we drove by Tony pointed to the hill and said, "We used to come here and sled a lot when we were kids." I looked out at the hill, barren-looking with a few faded fallen leaves blown across patches of winter grass. It was almost Thanksgiving and winter was definitely here.

"We still come sometimes," Tony added. "You like to sled?"

I shivered and shook my head, brushing back my hair. The car sped along and the sledding hill was behind us. "No," I said, "not since I read *Ethan Frome*."

"Another book!" There was just a trace of impatience in his voice.

I had read *Ethan Frome* for a book report the year before and had shed many tears for Ethan and Mattie Silver.

"It's a book about two people who went sledding down a hill," I said, "and ran into a tree to try to kill themselves."

"Sounds stupid to me," Tony said with a snort of laughter.

We had just reached the pathway down to the lake, and I got out of the car stiffly, clutching my Spanish book, my notebook, my purse, *Les Misérables*, and my European history book.

"Hey, Lorrie—what's the matter, what's the hurry?"

"Thanks for the ride," I said. I knew my voice trembled but I couldn't help it. I started to walk away and tried not to cry. I didn't want him to know that he had hurt my feelings.

"Hey, wait a minute. What did I say?" He got out of the car and caught my arm. I stood still, my eyes lowered so I wouldn't have to look at him. "I just thought you'd like to go sledding sometime," he said. "Come on, what's wrong?"

"You're always making fun of me and my books," I mumbled miserably. I was aware that he was still holding my arm and standing very close to me.

"Ah, come on, I was just teasing you. I didn't mean anything. Come on, don't be mad."

"All right," I said, with my eyes still lowered. "I'm not mad."

"Sure?"

I nodded, still looking down.

"Okay, then. Now go on home." He let go of my arm and I turned away quickly.

Behind me I could hear the car door slam, the motor start. I hope I never see him again, I thought as I stumbled along hugging my books.

And as it turned out I didn't see him for a long time. He stopped coming around to the bus stop and I started riding home on the bus again and pretending I didn't care.

# 8

The first snowfall came the weekend before Thanksgiving. It was a light snow, barely enough to cover the ground and rooftops, but as I watched late that Saturday afternoon the falling snow seemed to hold the promise of the beautiful winter to come. This was what Aunt Frances and I had been waiting for—our winter at Willow Lake was really beginning at last.

Sunday morning I walked across this thin covering of snow to take bread crumbs and suet to the bird feeders. Aunt Frances liked birds, and besides the two stone birdbaths at opposite ends of the lawn, she had hung bird feeders in the birch grove—four very popular feeding stations. The first one up in the morning was supposed to take out the birds' breakfast.

I sprinkled the bread crumbs and suet on the screens

secured in the trees and scattered on the ground what was left over. It didn't look like a good breakfast to me, but I guess the birds liked it. A scrawny-tailed gray squirrel hardly waited for me to leave before he pounced on the bread I had left. When I got back to the house Aunt Frances was up, watching through the kitchen window.

"There's that squirrel," she scolded. "Greedy thing."

It was the coldest morning we had had, and dark skies seemed to promise more snow to come. It made me think about sledding . . . and about Tony.

But it didn't snow any more before Thanksgiving. Aunt Frances watched the weather reports carefully every day, because Aunt Adele, Uncle William, and Barbara were going to drive out from New York for Thanksgiving, and Aunt Frances and I were looking forward to it as a special occasion, our first Thanksgiving at Willow Lake.

A few scattered flakes early Wednesday morning worried Aunt Frances. She frowned up at the sky. "There was no snow in the forecast today," she said reproachfully.

"This won't be much," Mr. Ramsey assured Aunt Frances. He came about eleven o'clock that morning to bring us some of Mrs. Ramsey's homemade cranberry sauce for our Thanksgiving dinner. It looked delicious; dark ruby red in a round glass jar.

"No, this won't be much," Mr. Ramsey repeated. "I haven't seen the right kind of moon yet for a big snow."

"You can tell about snow from the moon?" I asked. Mr. Ramsey never ceased to amaze me. Aunt Frances said he made it all up for fun, but I was never sure.

"Sure. I can tell about snow and lots of other things from the moon." He stood big and sturdy in our kitchen, the collar of his heavy winter jacket turned up, a thick leather glove stuck in each side pocket. His boots alone were tremendous, and he seemed to fill up the whole kitchen.

"What else can you tell from the moon?" I asked.

Aunt Frances made a funny face behind Mr. Ramsey's back, and I knew she thought he was telling another of his tall tales.

"When to get my hair cut."

That surprised me completely, and I couldn't help giggling. He caught Aunt Frances off guard, too. "Your hair?" She peered at Mr. Ramsey curiously.

"Won't grow as fast if it's cut at the right time of the moon. That saves money at the barber shop."

"I suppose it does." Aunt Frances couldn't argue with that.

"And what else?" I wanted to know.

"When to make business deals," Mr. Ramsey said. "You get into a business deal at the wrong time of the moon and you've got trouble."

I didn't care about business deals. I thought haircuts were more interesting.

"Are you talking about astrology?" Aunt Frances asked suspiciously. I knew she didn't believe in *that*.

"Nope." Mr. Ramsey drew the gloves from his pockets one at a time and put them on with ceremony. "I just know what's the right moon for things. The moon ain't right for snow yet, but it's coming. Going to be bad storms this winter."

I shivered with delight. We would be snowbound before the fire, just like I had imagined.

But I didn't want to be *too* snowbound. I wanted to get to school and maybe see Tony again.

"I'm glad to know it's not going to snow too much today," Aunt Frances said, to be polite.

Outside the flakes were still coming down, but they did seem to be letting up.

"This won't be anything," Mr. Ramsey said as he left, and it wasn't. By five o'clock that afternoon the Sinclairs had arrived, reporting clear roads all the way from New York City.

Uncle William presented us with a tremendous basket of fruit and nuts, covered with red cellophane; and Aunt Adele fluttered around, taking off her gloves and scarf and fur hat. But Barbara was quiet. I wondered if something was wrong, and I didn't have to wait long to find out.

"She didn't want to come," I heard Aunt Adele tell Aunt Frances. "She has a boyfriend, a young man she met at college. He lives in New York, so she wanted to stay in New York this weekend. I told her holidays are family days."

So Barbara had a boyfriend. A *new* boyfriend, I should say. The year before, when she was still in high school, she had gone steady with a boy almost the whole school year. They'd broken up just before the senior prom, so he had asked another girl to the prom and Barbara hadn't gone at all. She cried a lot over "that dreadful boy," as Aunt Adele called him. But now a whole new life was beginning for Barbara: college and a brand-new boyfriend.

Of course I wanted to hear all about her new boyfriend, and that night when we were getting ready for bed Barbara told me.

"His name's Eric," she said in a dreamy voice. "Eric Anders." She sighed happily, while I thought quickly and decided that Barbara Anders would be a pretty name if she ever married Eric.

"What does he look like?"

I wondered if Eric could be as handsome as Tony. Nobody was, I was sure.

"Well," Barbara began slowly. "He's got blond hair, kind of curly. And he's got light brown eyes—hazel, I guess you'd say."

I nodded agreeably. But I liked boys with dark hair and dark eyes now.

"He's about this much taller than me." Barbara held her hairbrush a few inches above her head.

"Where does he live?"

"That's the wonderful part," Barbara exclaimed. "He lives right in New York, not very far from us. That's why I wanted to stay in the city this weekend. We could have had such fun." She sighed.

I understood. What was Tony doing for the weekend? Was his brother's garage closed? Was the L&G Cafe closed? Was Tony out on a date with the redheaded waitress this very moment? What was he doing *now*, eleven o'clock Thanksgiving Eve?

I thought about all this in the back of my mind and still listened to Barbara without missing a word.

"At school," Barbara was saying, "lots of girls meet guys who don't live anywhere near them at home. So it gets complicated. But this is so perfect—except"—she flourished her hairbrush—"I'm not in New York this weekend."

"I'm sorry," I said. I really was. I wanted Barbara to

be back in the city with Eric.

Perhaps to get her mind off her own problems, she said, "How about you? Any cute boys at this new school?"

"Ohhh . . ." I shrugged vaguely, drawing out the word.

Barbara's eyes lit up and she leaned toward me, ready to listen. "There *is* somebody."

I didn't answer at once. Then I said, "Not exactly. Just, well, there is this boy who drives me home sometimes."

"Ah-*ha!*" Barbara laid her hairbrush on the bed and sat hugging her knees. Suddenly I wanted to tell her all about Tony Jordan. I wanted to tell her how I felt about him.

"He quit school," I said apologetically. "Aunt Frances doesn't like that much."

"That's not so important," Barbara said. "Maybe he'll go back someday."

"Maybe he will," I agreed. I thought Barbara was super not to make a big deal out of Tony quitting school.

I told her how I met him at Andy's when I was with Darlene. And then I asked her how she met Eric.

"He's in my chemistry class—and we've really got it, Lorrie, the *chemistry*, I mean." We both began to giggle. Life was wonderful at the moment, laughing and sharing secrets with Barbara.

She became restless as the weekend passed, though, as if she had never before realized how little there was to *do* at the lake. Sometimes she sat staring into the fire as though her thoughts were a million miles away, and I knew she was thinking about Eric. Finally on Saturday, after wandering aimlessly around the house most of the afternoon, she suggested that we go into Greenwood to a movie after supper. I thought that was a terrific idea. My thoughts flew ahead to *after* the movie: right across the street from the theater was the L&G Cafe, and maybe, if Barbara and I went there for something to eat after the movie, Tony would be there.

"A movie sounds great," I told Barbara.

We called the theater and learned that a western was playing. I didn't like westerns—at least I never had. But I wasn't about to miss this one.

"Who else wants to come?" Barbara asked. She didn't know about my plan for *after*, and that if everybody else came it would be ruined. Aunt Frances and Aunt Adele would not want to go to the L&G Cafe.

Uncle William perked up his ears when he heard the movie was a western. He'd seen every movie John Wayne ever made.

"It's not John Wayne." I tried to discourage Uncle William politely.

"Mom?" Barbara turned to Aunt Adele, but Aunt Adele shook her head. "Not me, darling. When I go to a movie I want to see some beautiful clothes, maybe a bit of scenery in Paris or Venice—not a bunch of horses galloping in the dust."

I could kiss you, Aunt Adele.

"I think I'll stay home, too," Aunt Frances decided; and Uncle William reconsidered and said, "You two gals go along."

My plan was safe!

But as we drove into Greenwood, I had the sudden awful thought that maybe Barbara wouldn't want to go to the cafe. I glanced over at her as we sped along in the cold, dark night. She was always dieting, and the L&G Cafe was no place to go just for a beautiful atmosphere. I decided to mention it enthusiastically as we came out of the movie. "Let's go to that place across the street, Barbara," I would say. "Everybody goes there after the movies."

But as we parked the car and walked along the parking lot aisle toward the theater I knew I couldn't sit through a whole long movie wondering if Barbara was going to say, "Let's just go home, Lorrie. I'm not really hungry."

It was too soon after supper to think of food, even for me, much less Barbara, but I couldn't stand the suspense.

"After the show we have to go to the cafe," I said with mock gravity.

"We do?" Barbara laughed.

"It's just over there." I pointed across the street. "It's part of going to a movie in Greenwood on Saturday night."

"All right, then." Barbara linked her arm in mine, took a look across the street at the humble little L&G, and added, "Let's live it up!"

The theater marquee flickered on and off, and everything seemed so different and adventurous at night. As we stood at the box office buying our tickets I wished Tony would come along and see me standing there and say, "Well, what are *you* doing here?"

But that didn't happen. We just got our tickets and went inside, and I could only hope things would be more exciting after the movie.

I wanted to see Tony, and yet I was afraid to. I didn't want him to think that I came to the cafe to spy on him and his girlfriend. I felt guilty as I steered Barbara across the street and into the L&G, and I was immensely relieved when she said, "This is a cute place."

The night had turned cold, and it was cozy and warm in the L&G. It was crowded, and I felt that my words were coming true: everybody did go there after the movie. Tony, however, was nowhere in sight.

As we slid into a booth and Barbara unbuttoned her coat she said, "I feel like eating a bowl of chili, if they have any."

"I think all places like this have chili," I said.

There were two waitresses behind the counter, and I waited to see which one would come over to our booth. It turned out to be Tony's girlfriend; I smiled at her a little but she didn't seem to remember me, so I didn't say anything.

"I know a boy who dates that waitress," I told Barbara after we had given our order for chili and Cokes.

I had wanted to tell Barbara all about Tony the night she'd told me about Eric; but now I didn't want to reveal that he was the one who was dating the waitress. I knew Eric Anders must be so very different. But still I wanted to talk about Tony, even if I didn't identify him to Barbara.

"This boy dates that waitress, and my girlfriend, Darlene, she's crazy about this boy and she's real mad because he dates this waitress."

Forgive me, Darlene.

Barbara smiled absently. I'm sure she wondered how we ever got on this subject.

"I don't see why my girlfriend Darlene should care. She has lots of boyfriends. But it's funny"—I laughed and waved my hand in what I hoped was a casual manner—"she just gets so mad when she thinks about this certain boy dating this waitress."

It was silly, but I kept talking about Darlene and the waitress and Tony.

Barbara smiled politely again, and fortunately it wasn't long before our order came.

I ate slowly, hoping Tony would come in. Every time the door opened I looked away, and then looked up casually to see who had come in.

"It's after ten," Barbara said at last, reaching back to pull her arms through her coat sleeves.

The door of the lunchroom opened and Tony came in.

Now that we were leaving!

I put on my coat slowly, and when Barbara got out her mirror and lipstick I did the same. Maybe we could stall for an hour or so. . . .

Tony didn't see us. He went to sit at the counter, and the redheaded waitress walked right over to him, poured him a cup of coffee, and looked back over her shoulder at the clock. I suppose she was almost through for the evening. Tony had come in to pick her up. Soon she would be riding along with him in his car, sitting where I sat when I rode with Tony. Only she wouldn't have a pile of books between them, as I always did. She'd be sitting right next to him. Maybe he'd have his arm around her shoulder.

"Ready to go?" Barbara asked.

After waiting and hoping that Tony would come in, it was suddenly very hard to get up and walk by the counter where he was sitting. I began to hope that Barbara and I could sneak out before he saw us. But he glanced up as we came by. He was surprised, and an expression of curiosity crossed his face. He hadn't expected to see *me* in town at night, I thought grimly. He probably thought I went to bed after supper, like a little kid.

But he spoke to me.

"Hi, kiddo," he said. The waitress glanced at me without interest.

"Hi," I answered, so softly he couldn't have heard me. And I couldn't have said another word if my life depended on it.

He didn't try to stop me or talk to me; and Barbara, walking ahead of me, didn't even realize that someone had spoken to me.

The waitress came down to the cash register at the end of the counter to take our money. Tony watched as we paid the check. I couldn't help looking back as we went out, and he was still watching. He saluted me as he had the first day I met him, and I wanted to tell him again that I wasn't really mad because he'd teased me about my books—at least I wasn't mad anymore.

# 9

On Sunday Aunt Adele, Uncle William, and Barbara drove back to New York; from there Barbara would return to college and Eric. Monday night it began to snow at Willow Lake. It snowed almost continuously for two days, and Aunt Adele called up from New York to say it was snowing there, too, and wasn't it lucky the snow had held off until after Thanksgiving, otherwise they never could have come to the lake. Barbara might not have agreed with that.

Following the snow there was an intense cold, which I felt most in the dark early mornings as I walked up to the highway to catch the bus.

The combination of snow and extreme cold formed a frozen crust on all the outdoor world. In the birch grove and the woods all the juncos and tiny brown sparrows came to the bird feeders in such numbers they covered the screens from sight and quickly ate them bare. "Oh, the poor dear birds," Aunt Frances said. "It's hard for them when everything is covered with snow."

By mid-December the lake was frozen and ice-skating began. The summer activities had concentrated around the lodge and Ramseys' pier, and in the winter the skating centered there, too. Mr. Ramsey built a fire on the bank on Saturday and Sunday afternoons. A few logs were pushed around the fire for people to sit on; and there were always children there, driven in from town by their parents or deposited there by weekenders who preferred to remain comfortably indoors at the lodge.

I didn't see Tony Jordan for about a week after the night Barbara and I went to the movie. The afternoons were short, and it was already getting dusky when I got to the bus station for the 4:20. I waited inside a nearby store because it was so cold, but I always stood by the door and kept a lookout in case Tony came driving along.

It seemed silly to stand there day after day, watching for someone who didn't come. Then one afternoon, there he was. He was parked in the bus zone when I came walking along.

"Remember me?" He leaned across the car seat to open the door for me on the passenger side.

"Sure I remember you," I kidded. "Isn't your name George?"

It was wonderful to be in the car again, warm and cozy, with headlights of other cars glowing brightly in the early twilight.

"I've been busy at the garage," Tony explained as we

sped along the highway. "Cold weather always brings a lot of dead batteries. People need a tow or a start with jumper cables. My brother always says if a car's got any problems, cold weather brings them all out."

I listened intently. His life was so different from mine. While I sat at school desks, he was out in the bitter cold getting cars to start.

"A car can get along in warm weather even if it's a heap of junk," Tony went on, gazing straight ahead at the oncoming traffic. "But as soon as this kind of weather comes, watch out."

"Oh, I know," I said wisely.

"If you don't see me so often, that's why." He glanced over and smiled at me. "How've you been?"

"Pretty good."

Well, not really all *that* good. Something always seemed to be missing from the days I didn't see him.

"Do you like working at the garage?"

"It's not bad." Tony shrugged.

"Do you ever think about coming back to school?"

There, I had finally asked the question that was so often on my mind.

Tony hesitated, and then to my surprise he said, "Yeah, sometimes I think about it—"

Oh, maybe he would come back!

"—but then I always figure what do I need it for?"

I wasn't sure what to say to that. I thought everybody ought to know what they needed school for. How was Tony ever going to "get ahead" or "amount to anything," as Aunt Adele would have said?

"I got better things to do than hang around places like

70

Andy's and worry about some dumb test coming up."

I had to stifle a giggle. Tony's impression of what going to school was like was so unexpected. Not classes, cafeteria, programs in the auditorium, gym. School for Tony had been hanging around snack shops with threats of tests spoiling his fun.

"What's so funny?"

I wasn't giggling, but I couldn't keep the smile from my face. "Oh, Tony, school is so much more than *that*."

"Yeah?" He looked at me skeptically. "Like what?"

I hunted around for the right words. "You know," I began hopefully, "school is learning things and having friends—it's kind of fun."

He shook his head with amazement. "You really mean that, don't you."

"Of course."

"Never seemed like that to me. Big pain in the neck. I'm glad I'm out."

There was something about the way he said this, just a bit too forcefully, that made me wonder for a moment whom he was trying to persuade, me or himself. Maybe sometimes he did think about going back and didn't want to admit that he had been wrong to quit. That would take courage. Some of the other guys might laugh at him for quitting and then coming back. He'd be a year behind all his classmates. It would be hard to do.

Anyway, for now he had said school was a big pain in the neck. There didn't seem to be anything more I could say after that.

"Come on, let's talk about something else," he said, reaching over to take my hand in his.

"Okay," I replied, and he gave my hand a little squeeze.

The cold weather continued and Tony was busy at the garage. It was almost Christmas before I saw him again. We were going to New York for Christmas, to Aunt Adele's. School ended on Friday for the two-week Christmas holiday, and by midmorning Saturday I was packed and ready to leave. Aunt Frances said it would be a couple of hours before we would be going, so I got on my jacket and went down by Ramseys' pier to skate. Tony came along about half an hour later, with Darlene and Steve. I had come up to sit on one of the logs near the fire to warm myself, and I was telling Mr. Ramsey about going to New York for Christmas. I could hardly think what I was saying when I saw Tony coming, and Mr. Ramsey turned around to see whom I was looking at.

"Here's Lorrie!" Darlene cried, wading through the snow to sit beside me on the log. She was bursting with excitement and kept nudging me, in case I hadn't noticed *who* was with her. "Steve and I went to the L&G to have some coffee and doughnuts before we came out here, and Tony was there—he still hangs around that waitress," she explained. "Anyway, Steve asked him to come along with us. Wasn't that nice of him!" She giggled, and I couldn't help feeling a pang of sympathy for Steve.

"Hi, Lorrie," Steve called to me as he came toward us. Tony only nodded at me silently.

While they put on their skates Mr. Ramsey hovered nearby and I never did finish telling him about going to New York for Christmas. Red-faced and probably frozen, he never deserted his fire. He helped the little kids with

72

their skates and gave out weather forecasts. Lights from a Christmas tree in the lobby shone through the lodge windows. It was easy to imagine "Jingle Bells" or "Deck the Halls" playing like background music in a movie.

"How've you been?" Tony asked me when Darlene skated off with Steve. She kept looking back at us and waving; she probably wanted to skate with Tony next.

"I've been fine."

"Still reading that sad story about the characters on the sled?"

"I read that last year," I said. "I was reading *Les Misérables*."

"Yeah, that's right." He seemed pleased with himself. "I remember now."

We stood awkwardly on the bank, Mr. Ramsey nearby slapping his hands together in their thick gloves.

"Come on," Tony said, and we went out on the ice and started to skate along, holding hands. We skated past the clusters of children, past Darlene, who had fallen on the ice and was looking decidedly unamused while Steve laughed and tried to pull her up again, past the end of Ramseys' pier, past the lodge.

"Oh," I said, "we're getting too far away."

"Too far away from what?" Tony asked. There was a cove in the lake bank, and we were hidden from the other skaters by a small promontory of land clustered with stubby fir trees. Tony stopped and stood looking down at me steadily, still holding my hands.

"We should go back to the others," I said, mostly to have something to say.

"Why?"

"Well—why?—I don't know why. . . ." I laughed self-consciously. Tony was still looking at me steadily, and I was sorry I'd come out without any makeup. The wind stung my eyes and made them watery, and my nose was probably red. I suddenly realized how cold it was and I began to shiver.

Tony looked away at last, across the lake. "Which house is yours?"

"Oh"—I turned and nodded my head—"that one there, the log house by the birch grove."

Tony stared at the house. "Nice place," he said softly.

"You'll have to come in sometime and meet my aunt," I said. "I—I know she'd like to meet you," I went on nervously. "She thought it was nice of you to drive me home—" I stopped.

He looked down at me and didn't say anything at first. After what seemed a long time he said again, "So how've you been?"

"Fine." I tried to draw my hands away, but he held them tightly.

"It's cold, Tony."

He didn't answer. Instead he bent his head toward mine and kissed me.

I had never thought the most wonderful moment of my life would come when my feet stung with cold and my hands felt numb.

He drew back and looked at me to see if I was mad or anything about the kiss, and when I smiled a little he seemed relieved and said, "Okay, now we can go back."

I didn't want to go back. I wanted to stay right where I was and freeze to death while Tony kissed me again. But I couldn't say that!

74

He started off, skating faster than I was used to skating, and I tried to keep up with him. But I was shaky with cold and the glory of his kiss, and when I felt myself falling, skidding down to the ice, I wasn't really surprised, only amazed that I hadn't fallen sooner. But Tony grabbed me so quickly I was up again almost at once. I was surprised to feel how strong he was, how easily he seemed to lift me, as though it were nothing at all.

"Are you all right?" His face was very close to mine, his dark eyes staring at me, a lock of dark hair falling across his forehead as usual.

"Yes—yes, I'm all right." I brushed at my clothes and felt clumsy and cold, and shakier than ever after falling. My knee hurt and tears came into my eyes. I didn't want Tony to see me crying.

"Are you crying?" he asked.

I shook my head. "It's just the wind. It's so cold—I don't know why it has to be so cold."

He took my hands again, and we skated back to the edge of the lake slowly.

Darlene and Steve were sitting on one of Mr. Ramsey's logs. "Oh, there you are!" Darlene called. Then, as Tony and I sank down on the log, she said, "I've got a great idea." I tried to rub my knee and brush the tears out of my eyes without letting anyone see.

"What's the matter with you?" Steve was watching me, but Darlene was concentrating on Tony and didn't notice.

"I'm just cold," I mumbled.

"I've got the most super idea," Darlene was saying again. "Let's all go to the pizza place out near the shopping center. I'm starved—how about you, Lorrie?"

75

Tony was watching me. I didn't care *where* we went, so long as we went together. It would be like a date, I thought, Darlene and Steve, Tony and me.

"How about it, Lorrie?" Darlene asked. "Can you come?"

It was the only time in my life that I can recall ever completely forgetting something, something *important*. At that moment I forgot that we were ready to leave for New York. "I'll ask my aunt," I said.

"How could you have forgotten?" Aunt Frances stared at me as if I might be coming down with something. How could I have forgotten—good question. I had only gone out to skate in the first place because I was all packed and ready to leave. I ran back down the steps to where Darlene and Steve and Tony waited, making snowballs to throw at the trees. I had asked them to come in, but they'd said their boots were all snowy and they'd wait outside.

"I can't come," I said to Darlene. I couldn't look at Tony. "We're going to New York for Christmas, we're leaving now."

"Oh." Darlene sounded disappointed. "Well, have a real nice Christmas."

"Yeah, Merry Christmas, Lorrie," Steve said.

"Merry Christmas," I answered. "Sorry about the pizza."

And then there wasn't any more reason for them to stay.

Tony said, "Merry Christmas, kiddo." As they started to walk away through the snow he looked back and touched his hand to his forehead in a salute. Then he was gone.

"I can't imagine how you could have forgotten," Aunt

Frances said again when I came back into the house.

"I don't know either—isn't it silly?" I said. The house already looked empty: our bags by the door, Aunt Frances's coat and scarf and gloves laid out on a chair, her handbag and keys on the table.

"I thought we'd have a sandwich before we go," Aunt Frances said, starting toward the kitchen. Through the front window I watched Steve and Darlene and Tony walking away down the Lake Road.

"What's the matter, Lorrie?" Aunt Frances paused in the kitchen doorway. "Why are you rubbing your leg?"

"Oh," I said. I hadn't even realized that I was rubbing my knee with cold, trembling fingers. "I fell on the ice and my knee hurts a little, but it's nothing, it's all right."

"I'm sorry you fell, dear."

"It's all right, really."

Tony Jordan had kissed me!

"Well, let's have our sandwiches," Aunt Frances said. "How about grilled cheese?"

"Sure." Darlene and Steve and Tony were out of sight now. I turned from the window and followed Aunt Frances into the kitchen.

"Not that we have much choice; cheese is about all we have to make sandwiches with," Aunt Frances said. The refrigerator was just about bare because we were going away for two weeks.

"Cheese is fine," I said. I wondered what the pizza place was like. I wanted to be there. I wanted to be there so much.

It began to snow more while we sat in the kitchen eating our sandwiches and drinking cocoa. And we drove into

New York under low, darkening skies. Tony had kissed me, and now I had to go away for two weeks. It seemed like an eternity.

# ❧ *10* ❧

Aunt Adele's apartment, which was fashionably close to Central Park, glittered and glistened with Christmas decorations. A giant tree stood in the bay window. Holly, mistletoe, and pine branches overflowed from vases, and brightly wrapped packages seemed to be everywhere.

There was a great deal of coming in and going out, telephones ringing, and an atmosphere of celebration and whirling activity. Uncle William occasionally looked a little weary from all this activity, but Aunt Adele was radiant.

Barbara, of course, was home from college for the holidays. She spent her mornings in jeans and her evenings in party dresses. Every night there was something going on. I went along sometimes. I went to two parties, a jazz concert, and a performance of *The Nutcracker Suite* ballet.

If I didn't want to be back at the lake instead, it would have been a terrific Christmas.

Barbara's boyfriend, Eric Anders, was really nice. He never made me feel left out. He was just about the way I had pictured he would be, and madly in love with Barbara. His father was the head of a large New York law firm, and I could easily see Eric, Jr., fitting into the firm when he had his law degree. Besides taking Barbara somewhere every night, he called her every morning on the phone and spent a lot of time lounging around Aunt Adele's apartment in the afternoons.

"He's almost like one of the family already, isn't he," Aunt Frances said to me one night when I had come into her room—Aunt Adele's blue-and-ivory guest room—to say good night.

"He is," I agreed. "He's nice, don't you think?"

"Yes—oh, yes, of course," Aunt Frances replied solemnly. "And Barbara seems very fond of him."

"I think *love* is the word, Aunt Frances."

Aunt Frances shook her head in wonder. "I can remember when she was just a little girl."

"Little girls grow up," I teased her, "even me."

"Oh, you!" she said, and gave me a playful swat on the behind.

On New Year's Eve, Barbara had a party. As far back as I could remember, Barbara had always had a party sometime during the holidays. I could trace the years of my life remembering Barbara's parties: the earliest ones when the little girls played together and the little boys had fights behind the sofas; later parties when the girls were gigglingly conscious of the boys and Aunt Adele swept around trying to organize games (when she left the room we played kissing games); and parties of more recent years, where everybody had a date, danced to Barbara's records, and kissed under the mistletoe.

Usually Barbara's parties were a day or so before or after Christmas, but this year her party was saved for New Year's Eve, and it was the most lavish of them all. Aunt Adele hired a catering service and the buffet and table in the dining room were ladened with all kinds of marvelous food. There were paper hats for everybody, and confetti and noisemakers. I had a new dress for the party, deep crimson with a flounced skirt and a scooped neckline just right for the gold necklace Aunt Adele had given me for Christmas. I put on gold-frost eye shadow and my new burgundy plum lipstick, and I was surprised at how good I looked.

I surprised Barbara, too. "Lorrie!" she exclaimed with delight. "You look *so* pretty."

You'll have lots of boyfriends someday, Darlene had said . . . Right now I only wanted one: Tony Jordan.

"That dress is just perfect for you," Barbara said enthusiastically.

"Thank you, my loyal fan." I picked up the edges of my skirt and made a grand, sweeping bow. "I'm so gorgeous I can't go outside; I would stop traffic and the whole city of New York would be in a panic."

Barbara laughed merrily, and I turned back to the mirror to admire myself some more. In the reflection of the mirror I could see Barbara behind me sitting on the edge of her bed, ready for the party, fastening the clasp of her bracelet. I was especially happy that night, because my

thoughts were already back at Willow Lake. I was thinking about wearing the crimson dress and wondering if
Tony would ever see me in it.

My date for the party was a friend of Eric Anders, a boy
name Charles. He had pale blue eyes and such a clean,
fair-skinned face that he looked like he'd been scrubbed
and polished just for the party; I smiled at him a lot as we
danced, which seemed to surprise him; he had probably
been told I was shy. But I couldn't help myself. I suppose
it was a combination of things, the general festivity of the
party, the beautiful new dress, the knowledge that the
two-week holiday was ending and we would soon be
going home, thinking about Tony Jordan seeing me in the
dress; all those things. I felt flushed and exhilarated, filled
with a sparkling-eyed happiness. I wanted to smile at
everybody!

"My, you're having a good time, aren't you, Lorrie?"
Aunt Adele said to me at one point during the evening.
She and Aunt Frances were standing in the archway between the living room and the dining room, watching both
the couples dancing in the living room and those who
wandered out to nibble on refreshments.

"It's a wonderful party," I said, and Aunt Adele patted
my shoulder with satisfaction and glanced over to see if
Aunt Frances was noticing what a good time I was having.

Aunt Frances had a thoughtful expression on her face,
and she smiled at me uncertainly. I realized why as I
started away and heard Aunt Adele saying to her, "See,
Frances, this is where Lorrie belongs, here in New York,
meeting these nice young people from good schools, good
families. See what a good time she's having. She's grow-

ing up, you know. It's a crime to keep her out at that desolate lake.'' But Aunt Adele had been suggesting things for me all my life, and her words were such familiar refrains that I had become like the people who heard the boy cry wolf so much they stopped listening.

When at last it was time for Aunt Frances and me to go back to Willow Lake, Aunt Adele said she thought she would come with us.

"It's such a let-down-feeling time of year, after the holidays," she said. "A little vacation will be just the thing." She packed up a supply of jewelry and several bottles of nail polish, and was prepared to rough it with us for a week or so. Aunt Frances was delighted and kept telling Aunt Adele how pretty the lake was with the snow and all; but I hardly thought about anything except that the two weeks were over and it was time to go back.

We got to Willow Lake late on a Saturday afternoon. I unpacked my things and restlessly tidied up my room, wishing Barbara were there so we could go into Greenwood for a movie and then to the L&G Cafe. Maybe Tony would be there.

Wouldn't that be wonderful! But I couldn't do it alone, and Barbara was miles away.

All around my room were the Christmas presents I had brought back from New York: the sweater from Barbara, ready for my first day back to school, a diary—what secrets would I write in it?—gloves and a scarf and a silver bracelet, a favor from a party I had gone to with Barbara and her boyfriend, the program from *The Nutcracker Suite*, some candy, the gold necklace from Aunt Adele, and the new dress I had gotten in New York.

I wondered what Tony and Darlene and Steve had been doing; if they had been coming out to the lake to skate. It made me feel forlorn to think that they had probably been right out there on the lake without me.

"Supper's ready, Lorrie," Aunt Frances called.

"Coming," I answered, and I put on the new silver bracelet and wore it down to supper.

A fire was crackling in the fireplace, and all over the house were signs of Christmas brought back from New York, gifts and boxes of candy, wisps of tissue paper and ribbons.

I was so happy to be back—and I couldn't know how soon everything was going to change.

## 11

It was funny, but somehow I had never thought of Aunt Adele ever meeting Darlene. Or Steve. They existed in a world so separate from Aunt Adele's world. But the day after we came back to the lake, on Sunday afternoon, I heard Aunt Frances calling to me from the foot of the stairs. "Lorrie, some friends of yours are here." As I came to the top of the stairs I could see Darlene and Steve and Tony standing inside the front door, and I could hear Aunt Adele saying, "Do come in and sit down. I'm Lorrie's Aunt Adele."

As I came down the stairs everyone looked up and seemed relieved to see me coming, the link that could join the two worlds.

I felt flustered as I introduced everyone. I was sure both my aunts could tell how special Tony was to me.

85

Darlene, Steve, and Tony looked as ill at ease as I felt, and Aunt Adele asked them again to sit down. "Take off your coats," she urged. "Warm up by the fire."

I knew she didn't want them to rush off before she got a good look at them.

"Let me fix you something," Aunt Frances offered. In New York she had always known all my girlfriends, and I never had any boys stop by to see me, so it was a rather new experience for her. Offering refreshments was her first thought.

"Oh, no thanks. We can't stay." Darlene kept glancing around the room, seemingly awed by everything she saw. "We just came to see if Lorrie wanted to come out with us for a while."

"But you mustn't hurry off," Aunt Adele protested, turning on the charm. "I've been wanting to meet some of Lorrie's new friends. Now you must sit down for a few minutes at least. Wouldn't you like some hot chocolate—or some coffee—*something?*"

"No—no, thanks," Steve answered. They were all polite, but they seemed to feel awkward, perhaps because both my aunts were staring at them, or perhaps just because they had never been in my house before. They had probably thought they'd just stop by and see if I wanted to go out with them, and they hadn't expected to be trapped by my aunts.

"Gee, this is a nice place, Lorrie," Darlene said.

"Yeah, it's real nice," Steve echoed. I liked him, I thought; Darlene ought to be nicer to him and not flirt with Tony—or any other boys, as she sometimes did.

"And you're the young man who drives Lorrie home

from school sometimes, aren't you?'' Aunt Frances was saying, and I wondered what my aunts had thought Tony would be like. I was sure they couldn't have expected him to be so handsome.

"Yes, ma'am,'' Tony said.

Aunt Frances wasn't sure what to say after that, and when nobody else said anything right away, Darlene repeated, "Gee, this sure is a nice place.''

I could imagine Aunt Adele wincing inwardly, and I wondered why I had never noticed before that Darlene started so many sentences with "gee.''

"Why don't you show your friends around, Lorrie?'' Aunt Frances suggested. "There isn't much to see''—she turned to the three of them—"but you might like to look around. This was just a place for the summer when I bought it, but we fixed it up and had a furnace put in.'' She was herding them to the doorway of the kitchen, and they stood beside her, peering into the kitchen. I was so glad all the lunch dishes were washed and put away.

Then Aunt Frances said, "But Lorrie can show you around. Show them my studio, Lorrie.''

"It's over here,'' I said, and they all trooped after me, across the living room again, to the door of Aunt Frances's studio. I was grateful to see Aunt Adele and Aunt Frances going back to their chairs by the fireplace.

"This is where my Aunt Frances paints,'' I said.

None of them seemed to want to go past the doorway as they stood looking into Aunt Frances's cluttered room strewn with paints and canvases.

"Come on in,'' I said, and they followed me cautiously. There was a half-finished painting on the easel, a painting of the lodge and the promontory of land dotted with the little fir trees. They all looked at it and Darlene said, "Gee, is she ever good."

I had grown up in rooms littered with art supplies and half-finished pictures on easels, but it was an unfamiliar world to them. Darlene gingerly touched a few things on Aunt Frances's table, brushes and tubes of oils; Steve looked around as though hoping to find the nearest exit; and Tony just looked at me.

"Where's your room, Lorrie?" Darlene asked.

"Upstairs. Would you like to see it?"

Darlene nodded. "I'd love to, if it's all right."

"Sure it's all right," I said. I was glad that Steve and Tony said they'd wait for us; I couldn't see myself leading them on a tour upstairs. Darlene clumped up the stairs after me, saying that she should have taken her boots off; but I told her the boots were all right.

When we got to my room Darlene said, "Oh, Lorrie, this is a darling room! It must be great to have a room of your own. I have to share, you know."

"With Anna May?"

"Yeah." Darlene made a face. "I wish she'd get married and then I could have the room to myself. I wouldn't care, she never lets me wear any of her clothes anyway."

"That's too bad," I said sympathetically.

"She's so stingy," Darlene said.

Some of my Christmas presents were still out on the window seat and dresser top, and Darlene admired them—particularly the sweater Barbara had given me and my new jewelry. She loved my new dress and held it up in front of herself by the mirror to see how it would look on her. With her dark hair, she would have looked better in it than I did. I picked up my bathrobe and a stack of books from the chair by my bed and tried to make it look as though I usually didn't let books and stuff stack up on chairs.

"It must have been swell spending Christmas in New York," Darlene said wistfully.

"I'm glad to be back," I told her, but she hardly understood *that*.

As we went downstairs I saw that Aunt Frances and Aunt Adele had at last succeeded in getting Steve and Tony to sit down, and they looked relieved to see Darlene and me coming back. They stood up quickly, and Steve said, "Well, we've really got to go now." I think Aunt Adele made him nervous.

"I guess we better," Darlene said. "We're going sledding, Lorrie. Can you come?"

Then Tony said, "Lorrie doesn't like sledding."

In the moment of silence that followed, everyone looked at him and then at me, uncertainly, waiting to see what I would say.

"Don't you like sledding, dear?" Aunt Frances asked vaguely. I suppose she was wondering how she had raised me all these years and never known I didn't like sledding—or, perhaps, *why* I didn't like sledding, as I had never gone sledding.

I couldn't look at Tony. How could he have said that? I was overcome with embarrassment. "I'll come and watch," I said, and everybody laughed as though what Tony said had only been a joke after all. I ran to get my jacket.

"Now, come again," Aunt Frances called after us as we left.

"Your aunt is real nice, Lorrie," Darlene said as we walked toward the car. "I always pictured her different."

"How?" I asked.

"Oh, I don't know. More stern, I guess."

"I told you she wasn't stern," I began, but Darlene was saying:

"And your other aunt—wow, is she ever glamorous."

"Yes, she's very glamorous," I agreed.

"Is she the one you went to visit in New York?"

I nodded, and Darlene sighed contentedly. "She sure is glamorous."

They had driven out from town in Tony's car. It was so good to see it again, a slightly worn but dear old friend, and I got in the front seat beside Tony, remembering all the times I had been afraid I would never ride in it again. As he started the engine Tony looked over at me for a moment as if he, too, was thinking it had been a long time since I'd sat there beside him. I looked away quickly, without saying anything to him. I didn't think he ought to have said anything about my not liking sledding; crying over *Ethan Frome* wasn't something I wanted the whole world to know.

When we got to the hill there were about a dozen or so sledders there already; everybody seemed to be having a lot of fun. Darlene and Steve wouldn't believe that I was serious about only watching. They laughed and teased me, and finally they gave up and went up the hill, dragging the sled behind them. Tony and I watched from the foot of the hill. I wanted to say, "How could you say I didn't like sledding, in front of everybody!'' but when I looked up at Tony he was smiling at me with his lazy, amused smile, and I couldn't be angry with him.

Darlene and Steve shrieked and waved to us from the top of the hill; and then we watched them fly down across the snow—faster, faster, faster—tumbling off into the snow at the foot of the hill. It didn't look at all dangerous or frightening. If Tony asks me to go down the hill with him, I'll go, I thought. But he didn't ask me. He leaned back against a tree trunk and seemed to forget that I was there, as we watched Darlene and Steve drag the sled up the hill again.

When I had just about decided Tony really had forgotten I was there, he looked at me and then reached out and took my hand, drawing me closer to him.

"Remember what you said about liking winter best?" he asked.

Of course I remembered, but I was surprised that he remembered after all this time. It had been such a casual conversation, the very first time he had ever driven me home.

"It still is my favorite," I said.

"You know, I can kind of see why," he said, glancing around at the snowy woods. A little flock of sparrows flew out from the trees at the foot of the hill, and we watched for a moment as they circled and found new branches to light upon.

"It's got a certain . . ." He paused, baffled for the right word.

"Atmosphere?" I offered.

"Yeah, that's it. It's got a certain atmosphere."

He knew how I felt! He *understood*.

Then he put his arm around my shoulder and teased, "Sure, winter's okay. I get to keep pretty girls warm." I knew he was only teasing because being serious embarrassed him. And that was all right. That was something *I* understood. And it was good to feel his arm around me.

"I *am* cold," I admitted, leaning closer to him.

"We can sit in the car," he said. "We can watch just as well from there."

"You don't have to just watch," I said. "Why don't you go? Go with Darlene?" I added recklessly. He just laughed and, still holding my hand, started back to the car. We got in and he let the engine run so that we could listen to the radio and have the heater on. I thought maybe he would ask me how my trip to New York was or if I'd had a nice Christmas. But he didn't say anything at all. He kissed me. And then he kissed me again.

He drew back after the second kiss, and we sat holding hands. The radio was playing a love song. It was just like a scene on TV or something. And it was happening to *me*.

"Do you really think I'm pretty?"

"Did I say that?" He was teasing me again. He liked to tease me, and I liked to have him tease me.

I looked up at him from lowered lashes. "You said you got to keep pretty girls warm in winter."

"Oh, yeah, that's right. I did say that, didn't I."

I waited forever for him to go on.

"Sure, you're pretty," he said sort of gently, "and you're kind of . . . well, kind of different."

I hoped that was good. "What do you mean different?"

Again he couldn't seem to find the right words. "Just

different . . . you know, with all your books, and you look scared all the time. Well, not scared, that's not what I mean. Shy. You always look kind of shy, like you need somebody to take care of you. Know what I mean?''

He really was trying to describe exactly what he felt. I knew I was shy, so I couldn't argue with that; and if he wanted to take care of me, that was okay with me. Some boys might have been more eloquent, but I thought Tony Jordan was saying everything just about as well as it could be said.

When Darlene and Steve finally came back to the car, their faces were red with cold. Their breath was frosty in the air as they dragged the sled around to the back of the car and put it in the trunk. Darlene's dark hair tumbled from her red knit cap, and I thought she looked really pretty. Before they got into the car they had a brief snowball fight, and Steve chased Darlene when she tried to hide behind trees to get away from his snowballs.

"I'm starved," Steve announced as he pulled open the back door of the car and Darlene scrambled in brushing snow from her gloves.

"Let's go to the pizza place," Darlene said, to my delight. I was going to get to have pizza with them after all, even though I had missed out that other time.

The place was called Vittorio's. It was a large rustic place with a huge fireplace and stuffed birds decorating the walls. Not at all what I had expected. More like a hunting lodge than a pizza parlor. The floor was bare planks, and the tables had been scarred with knife-carved initials, hearts, and names. The fireplace created a marvelous atmosphere of warmth and comfort, and I sat waiting for the pizza in a delicious glow of happiness. Tony tilted his chair on the back legs and glanced around, nodding now and then as he saw someone he knew across the room.

"Do you come here a lot?" I asked.

"You could say that," he replied.

And now I was here, too. I was beginning to be a part of his life.

When I got home, Aunt Adele murmured something about how nice my friends were, though I knew she would never want Barbara dating a boy who had quit school; nor would she want Barbara to have a best friend who chewed gum and started so many sentences with "gee."

Aunt Frances said wasn't it nice they had come by for me; I had the definite feeling the two of them had been talking about us while we were gone. I could almost hear the conversation, with Aunt Frances saying, "See, Adele, Lorrie isn't cut off from the world here. She has friends." And Aunt Adele saying thoughtfully, "Yes, but are they really the right kind of friends? A boy who quit school, a girl like Darlene?" And Steve, what could she say about Steve? That he wasn't Eric Anders, Jr. I felt a sad, half-impatient helplessness that Steve's father didn't own a New York law firm.

On Monday school started again, the slow, halfhearted way everybody feels about coming back after a holiday. The Christmas tree in the main hall by the auditorium had been taken down, as well as other decorations, and the corridors had a cheerless, bare quality, like places do after holidays.

But *my* day wasn't cheerless. Tony was in Andy's after

94

school, sitting in a booth with Steve when Darlene and I walked in.

"I thought you didn't like hanging around places like this," I said, when Darlene and Steve left for a minute to talk to someone in another booth.

Tony looked at me with a teasing smile. "I said I didn't like hanging around worrying about homework and tests, stuff like that. Otherwise"—he spread his hands— "otherwise, it's not so bad."

I wanted to say, "School's not so bad, either," but I didn't. I knew I couldn't force Tony to come back to school.

Then Darlene was back, sliding into the booth across from me. Steve was close beside her, pulling a strand of her hair playfully.

We left Andy's together, all four of us, and walked to Tony's car. He was going to drive Darlene and Steve home, and then me. Some kids ran by dragging a small thrown-away Christmas tree they had probably found in an alley behind somebody's house. Bits of tinsel stuck to the scrawny, dried-up branches.

"Another Christmas is over," Darlene said wistfully. Our eyes met and I smiled. I knew just how she felt. Except this year I had been eager to have Christmas over so I could get back to Willow Lake. Next year would be different, I hoped. I wondered where we would all be when next Christmas came.

When we got to Tony's car he showed us where someone had dented its side, opening a car door in a grocery store parking lot. I didn't think it was too bad, but Steve and Tony talked about it like it was a big deal.

"These guys and their cars," Darlene whispered as we stood shivering and waiting to get in the car while Tony and Steve studied the scratches and the dent.

"I drove my mother to get groceries," Tony was telling Steve. "Good deed for the day, right? And this was my reward."

Steve clapped Tony on the back and they both laughed.

"Boys are nutty," Darlene told me. She shifted her purse and gave Steve a poke in the back. "Let's get in the car, huh? I'm freezing."

Steve and Darlene got in the backseat, and I sat up in front with Tony. I turned and looked back at Darlene once, and she gave me a wink that meant, I think Tony likes you. Maybe he's forgetting about the redheaded waitress at the L&G Cafe. Darlene could put a lot into one wink. I grinned back, which meant, I hope you're right.

Then I turned forward again and watched the road. I thought about Tony taking his mother to the grocery store. Another part of his life opened up to me as I pictured him helping his mother, pushing the cart for her in the store, lifting the grocery bags into the car. Everybody went to grocery stores; even carefree, out-of-school Tony Jordan.

When I got home from school that day Aunt Adele was surprised that it was so late. "Goodness, it's nearly five o'clock," she said. "Do you always have such late classes, dear?" Her question was put so innocently that I fell into it like a little animal stepping into a leaf-covered trap in the forest.

"Tony drove me home. We were talking."

"My goodness." Aunt Adele adjusted an earring. "All this time?"

And kissing, I thought, but I couldn't say that to Aunt Adele—or to Aunt Frances, who was coming from the kitchen just then, wearing an apron over her smock and carrying a large measuring cup.

"Ah, you're home, Lorrie. We were just beginning to wonder about you." She glanced at Aunt Adele apologetically, then hurried on to say that she was trying a new recipe for supper and she hoped we were both in daring moods because it didn't seem to be coming out just the way she had expected. But under her chatter I detected a note of doubt and unhappiness.

I went to hang my things in the closet; and even though I sensed that my aunts weren't too pleased about it, I couldn't help being happy about riding home with Tony again after all these weeks.

"Well," I had said to him in my best imitation of Darlene's airy manner, "I thought you'd given up driving me home."

"I thought I had, too," he'd said, and then he had reached over, taken my hand, and held it all the way to Willow Lake. When he'd stopped the car, he had still held my hand and we'd talked for a while. Just before I'd gotten out of the car, he'd kissed me good-bye.

"See you tomorrow," he'd said.

It was hard to come from that world, my world with Tony, back to the world of Aunt Adele and Aunt Frances. I was sure they wouldn't think it was a good idea for me to be sitting in a car at the side of the highway kissing a boy I'd never even had a single date with. Maybe I could count the afternoon we watched Darlene and Steve sledding as a date; or was that just "going out with the crowd"?

Anyway, I felt I had done something my aunts wouldn't approve of, and I tried to be extra helpful to make up for it. After I had hung up my jacket I went out to the kitchen and looked at what Aunt Frances was cooking. "That looks just super, Aunt Frances," I said. "I can tell just by looking that it's going to be delicious. And it smells wonderful."

Then I took some plates out of Aunt Adele's hands and said, "Why don't you sit and rest, Aunt Adele. I'll set the table."

I bustled around, trying to be very helpful and cheerful, as though somehow by this I could make them understand how nice Tony was. But as cheerful as I tried to be, there was a strain among the three of us as we sat down to supper, and we all seemed to be trying to think of unimportant little things to say to keep the conversation going.

While we were eating, a dreadful wind began to blow outside, and Aunt Frances said, "I think it's going to storm."

As the evening passed, the wind grew more wild and raging, until by bedtime both Aunt Frances and Aunt Adele were looking out into the night with increasing concern. A freezing rain had begun, and the trees in the birch grove and the woods bent and shuddered under the lashing of the wind and icy rain. Something outside at the back of the house came loose and banged against the wall. Aunt Adele laughed nervously and said she wondered if it was safe to go to bed. Actually, I didn't go to bed. I sat by the window in my room with the lights out, holding my robe close up to my chin as though some of the cold outside had come in through my window. I watched the terrible tearing wind and what I could see of the rain as it slashed through the light from the lamppost at the corner of our lawn and the gravel drive. Across the lake the lodge lights were almost lost from sight.

I had only meant to sit by the window a little while, but I must have dozed off, and I was awakened much later by a loud crash from the direction of the porch. At first, opening my eyes, I could hardly remember where I was. Beyond my window everything was completely black. There was no light by the drive, no lights showing at all from the lodge, just a tremendous blackness everywhere and the high screeching sound of the wind. I heard a noise in the hallway, so I got up, felt my way in the darkness across my room, and opened my door. Aunt Frances was standing beside her doorway, a lighted candle in her hand.

"I couldn't sleep," she said, and motioned with the candle. "The power lines must be down. I had to light this candle."

"What was that noise downstairs?" Aunt Adele's voice called to us waveringly through the darkness.

"I think a branch must have hit the house. On the porch, I think," Aunt Frances answered calmly. "Now don't be frightened, Adele. I've got a candle and we'll go down and see."

Aunt Adele came into the flickering range of light shed by Aunt Frances's candle, and we started down the stairs slowly, following Aunt Frances.

"It's cold down here," Aunt Adele said.

"Yes, it *is*," Aunt Frances agreed. "Well, of course, I should have realized. If the power lines are down the furnace is off as well as the lights."

"We can build a fire," I said. I thought it was the most exciting thing that could happen, to be so cut off and alone in the midst of the terrible storm.

"I think we'll have to," Aunt Frances said.

We went through the living room and looked out onto the porch. Aunt Adele, especially, was stunned at what we could see of the birch tree lying across the porch in a litter of screen and broken wood. "Frances, this is dreadful," she whispered, and at that moment whatever had come loose at the back of the house began banging again. Aunt Adele clasped her hands together and stepped back from the window to be well out of the way should there be any more falling trees.

Aunt Frances brought more candles from the kitchen and set them around the living room. The clocks had stopped, but I still had my watch on. "It's four o'clock," I said.

"It won't be long till morning, then," Aunt Frances said cheerfully. "We'll make a fire and be warm in a minute."

She went over to the fireplace. "Here, Lorrie," she said, "come and hold this candle for me."

For a moment before she handed me the candle, I caught a glimpse of her kindly plump face illuminated in the shadows. She had an expression of pleased excitement, like the excitement I felt; and I smiled at her as I took the candle.

When she had the fire started we sat down close around it, because Aunt Adele said she didn't think it was wise for us to go upstairs again. I think she believed the next falling tree might come straight through the roof into our bedrooms. But I wasn't frightened, and I don't think Aunt Frances was frightened. I curled up on one of the sofas and watched the firelight. After a while, I fell asleep, quite contented. Already I had almost forgotten the tension I had felt after school.

In the morning I was awakened by Mr. Ramsey pounding on the door and Aunt Frances padding across the floor in her bedroom slippers to let him in. I could see the tree across the porch and several others down across the lawn. Then I saw that everywhere, even on the frozen lake, were torn-down trees or parts of trees; and on everything else was a glittering, magical coat of ice, a world as sparkling as any of the decorations of the sparkling Christmas just past.

Mr. Ramsey had come to see if we were all right.

"Now you've had a real taste of what winter's like here," he announced proudly, nodding around at us.

"We certainly have," Aunt Frances answered, laughing.

Aunt Adele didn't look like she wanted to linger around for a second taste, but she smiled politely at Mr. Ramsey, and for a time at least, the strain we had felt the afternoon before was forgotten as everybody talked about the storm.

# 12

We were confined to the house that day and the next. All the roads in the area were slick with ice and covered with fallen branches and trees. The schools were closed, and there was a heavy snowfall the night after the ice storm. Aunt Adele thought Aunt Frances and I were crazier than ever to want to live permanently at Willow Lake.

The tree was removed from the porch, the electricity came back on, the loosened basement shutter that had been banging was fixed, and Aunt Frances tried to reassure Aunt Adele that there was nothing to worry about. "New York City has bad storms, too," she reminded Aunt Adele. Aunt Adele didn't feel that there was any comparison at all between a big city and a desolate lake during a storm.

When the roads were cleared, Aunt Adele took the first available train back to civilization.

That was Thursday. It was also the day the schools in Greenwood reopened, and when I got home from school that afternoon Aunt Frances had already returned from driving Aunt Adele to the train. She asked me to come and sit down in the living room for a minute.

"Well," she began brightly, but she sounded nervous. "Adele's safely off to New York."

I nodded and waited, a little curious as to why Aunt Frances seemed nervous.

"You know," she continued, "your Aunt Adele is worried about us." She laughed, to show me how silly she thought this was.

"You mean because of the storm?"

"Partly." Aunt Frances paused. "Of course it's just plain nonsense, but you know she never was too pleased with the idea of our living here."

Well, I certainly knew *that*.

Aunt Frances examined the print of her dress carefully. "But it's not just the weather and the storm," she said at last. "You know, Lorrie, Adele has always thought you should go to Lynden Hall, as Barbara did. She wants to be sure we do what's best, what your mother and father would have wanted. Adele thinks you would have more advantages at a school—"

"But I don't want to go to Lynden Hall," I interrupted so sharply it surprised even me. Aunt Frances looked up, startled.

"Don't get so excited, dear," she said. "It's just Adele's way. She can't help telling people what she thinks is best. You know she means well; it's because she loves you that she cares."

"But Aunt Frances—"

She held up her hand for me to wait. "I told Adele there will be plenty of time, goodness knows, when you're ready for college, for you to go away to school. I told her it's company for me to have you with me now. I love you very much, Lorrie, just as if you were my own child." She cleared her throat and hurried on. "But you know, dear, sometimes I wonder if I'm really doing the right thing. It's not easy to raise a child, and sometimes"—she seemed unwilling to look at me and examined the pattern on her dress again—"sometimes I wonder if Adele isn't right, at least about some things. Do you understand?"

"No, I don't. I like living here and going to Greenwood High School better than I'd like Lynden Hall."

"Do you, dear?" Aunt Frances smiled. "I'm glad. Sometimes I do wonder." Then she recalled that she hadn't yet finished what she had set out to say. She cleared her throat again and continued. "Well, now, anyway, Adele is a little worried about you. She doesn't think you've met . . . well, let's say, the right kind of friends."

Aunt Frances said this with a touch of regret that perhaps it really was true: I hadn't met the right friends. Out of a whole great big school, I hadn't met the right friends.

I was afraid to mention Tony, but I said, "Darlene's so nice, Aunt Frances, really she is. She's been so nice to me."

"I'm sure she has." Aunt Frances folded a neat small

crease in the skirt of her dress, edging it in with her fingernail. "But, for example, this going to that place with her after school."

"Andy's? What's wrong with that?"

Aunt Frances continued, and I could see she had thought out everything very carefully before speaking to me. "I've been thinking maybe that's holding you back from meeting some of the other girls at school, having more friends. Couldn't you go with some of the other girls who go to this place, instead of just going with Darlene all the time?"

I tried to imagine butting uninvited into another group. Aunt Frances didn't seem to understand how things were at school. Everybody had his own group.

"You know what I mean, dear"—Aunt Frances looked at me hopefully—"get to know some of the other girls at school."

We had never been so out of communication with each other before. Aunt Frances didn't understand how things were, and I couldn't understand why she thought that now, after almost five months at Greenwood High School, I could suddenly start going around with a whole new group of girls. Things just weren't like that. And even if they were, how could she expect me to drop Darlene, my very best friend?

"Perhaps you could invite some girls out here some Saturday for a little luncheon," Aunt Frances went on. "We should have done something like that sooner. It was my fault for not thinking of it." (I was sure that she hadn't thought of it even now; I could sense Aunt Adele behind this luncheon—menu and all.) "I was busy getting the house organized,'' Aunt Frances continued, "and finding someone to clean, and then with painting.'' She gestured wearily. "Well, I do get preoccupied, as Adele says.''

I didn't know what to say. I hated this whole discussion. I didn't want to have it anymore.

"Don't you think that would be a good idea, Lorrie? About the lunch, I mean. After all, it's not too late.''

"What do you mean, it's not too late?''

"I just mean that there's no reason why things can't be different. Maybe we just didn't get off to the right start here. And then there's this boy, Tony. By the way,'' she interrupted herself, "did he drive you home today?''

"Yes.''

Aunt Frances sighed. "I really don't think it's a good idea for you to see so much of him. After all, dear, a boy who quit school and all. It was nice of him to drive you home, but you could just say I prefer you to take the bus and I'm sure he'd understand.''

"I couldn't do that! He wouldn't understand at all!''

"Oh, I think he would.''

How did she know!

I tried to stay calm. "He's really very nice, Aunt Frances. You just don't know him. If you got to know him, you'd like him, I know you would.''

"I think I know enough, Lorrie.'' She stiffened a little, but I rushed on, not quite so calmly, clutching at straws.

"Maybe . . . maybe I could be a good influence on him, like Mrs. Peck said.''

Aunt Frances looked at me steadily. "Do you really believe that, Lorrie?''

I had no answer. I glared at her for a moment, then

106

lowered my eyes, and Aunt Frances said, more gently, "Don't look so unhappy, dear. I'm sure Tony will understand. Well, now"—more brightly—"let's not talk about it anymore right now, dear. You be thinking about whom you'd like to invite to the luncheon."

I went up the stairs to my room, confused and close to tears.

I couldn't really believe that Aunt Frances was as serious as she sounded. Surely now that Aunt Adele was gone Aunt Frances would soon lapse back into her usual easygoing ways. At supper we talked about other things, and by the next morning I even began to imagine that Aunt Frances had already forgotten.

But that afternoon she was watching for me after school, and she wanted to know if I had been to Andy's with Darlene and if Tony Jordan had driven me home. She was like a stranger compared to the Aunt Frances who had looked up from her letter that October afternoon and murmured absently, "Tony Jordan. That's a nice name."

"Yes," I said. "I went to Andy's with Darlene. Oh, Aunt Frances, what else could I do? She's my friend."

"But, Lorrie, didn't you even try?"

"How can I just suddenly say, 'No, I can't go to Andy's with you anymore'? How can I hurt her feelings?"

"I certainly didn't intend that you hurt her feelings."

"But it would. Everybody has their own special crowd. You can't just . . . well, just invite yourself."

"You could invite one of the other girls to go with you."

I couldn't picture myself marching up to any of the girls at school, girls I knew only casually to nod to or smile at when we passed in the halls, and saying, "Let's have a Coke together after school." Even if I didn't have Darlene for a friend, I was too shy to go up to girls I hardly knew and ask them to go to Andy's with me or come to lunch at my house some Saturday.

As for Tony, I said again that I couldn't just tell him I didn't want any more rides home.

"Well, Lorrie, whether you think you can or not, I have asked you not to see this boy." Aunt Frances's voice trembled, although she was trying to sound firm. "He's not the sort of boy—"

"But he *is* nice, really he is. He's not wild, like Mrs. Peck said. He—he wants to build a house someday, right here at Willow Lake."

Aunt Frances was not impressed. Her mouth tightened and she shook her head. "Lorrie, you just aren't listening to me."

"Yes, I am."

And I *was* trying to listen, to understand, but suddenly I was frightened. I knew that Aunt Frances was thinking about Lynden Hall. How could everything change so suddenly, overnight, just since Christmas? I had been so happy then.

Aunt Frances turned away wearily, gazing out across the snow-covered world and the frozen lake. Following her gaze, I saw Willow Lake streaked with long shadows of trees in the fading late afternoon sunlight.

I could not leave Willow Lake. I just had to stay.

## *13*

Aunt Frances was quiet but not unfriendly at breakfast Monday morning, and I set off for school determined to do the best I could. I knew just what times of the day Darlene went to our locker, and I went to the locker when I knew she wouldn't be there. After my last class I went to the library to study and I didn't see her the whole day.

Tony didn't come by the bus stop to drive me home. I waited, cold and shivering and miserable, sure he would come along at the last minute, but he didn't. I got on the bus, bewildered and unhappy. All day I had been bracing myself to tell him I couldn't ride home with him—and then he hadn't even showed up.

Aunt Frances was pleased. "Well, you're home nice and early today," she said approvingly. "Did you come on the bus?"

"Yes I came on the bus. And I didn't go to Andy's, either.'' I was suddenly tired; it had been the longest, most unhappy day I had ever spent, and I felt like bursting into tears. As I began fumbling with the buttons on my jacket I heard myself blurting out, ''I hope you're satisfied.''

"Lorrie!" Aunt Frances's pleasant, smiling face crumpled as if I had struck it. I looked down at my jacket stubbornly. Was I never going to get the buttons undone? I blinked back the tears that sprang to my eyes, and I wouldn't look at Aunt Frances as I took off my jacket at last and hung it in the closet.

"Lorrie," Aunt Frances said then, "I didn't mean you couldn't ever go to Andy's, if you enjoy it so much. I just meant that it would be better not to go *all* the time with the same girl. Get to know some other girls, too, dear."

"If I can't go with Darlene, I don't want to go," I said crossly. When I got up to my room I felt bad about hurting Aunt Frances on top of all my other problems.

I dreaded going to school Tuesday. My dumb plan was to go on trying to avoid Darlene. I should have known that wouldn't work for long. She had missed me Monday and came around to the library looking for me after school. I was sitting near the windows, looking out across the school grounds where the snow was melting in spots under the warmth of the bright January sun.

"Hey, Lorrie, I've been looking for you. Aren't you coming to Andy's?" Darlene had her fur jacket on and a knit cap with a pom-pom on top. She slid into the chair next to me, whispering and ducking her head away from the teacher who was sitting at the library desk.

"Not today," I whispered back. "I have to write this history paper."

"Oh, come on." She tugged at my arm, then frowned.

"Is anything wrong?"

"No, of course not," I whispered. The teacher looked up a moment, then went back to checking some reports or something on her desk.

"Where were you yesterday?" Darlene whispered.

"Oh—I was here."

"I saw your coat in the locker. Why didn't you come to Andy's?"

"I had to study."

"Well, then you need a break today," she joked, reaching over and closing the book I had opened before I'd started staring out of the windows. "Come *on*."

I had tried. I got up from the table, stuck my pencil in my purse, and picked up my books. I had tried, maybe only twice, but enough to know it wasn't going to work, at least not the way Aunt Frances wanted.

The teacher looked up again as Darlene and I left the library. Steve was waiting in the hall. "Oh, you found her," he said; it was good to see him standing there and to know that they had cared about finding me.

And later, while I was standing by the curb watching for the bus, Tony came driving up, and I knew I could never tell him I wouldn't go with him.

"I got tied up working with my old man yesterday," he said as I got into the car. It was the first time he had ever offered me an explanation of his time.

"Why so quiet, kiddo?" he asked as we drove along the street. I tried to think of something to say. We were passing the L&G Cafe, and the only thing I could think to say was, "You forgot to honk."

He looked at me curiously a moment, then reached over and took my hand. "Hey, come on, cheer up. You don't look very glad to see me."

"Of course I'm glad to see you." I let him hold my hand, but I looked straight ahead, wondering how I could tell him that I wasn't supposed to be here, riding along with him, holding hands. I was supposed to be on the bus.

A bit farther on he let go of my hand and reached into his jacket pocket. He took out a small white paper bag and dropped it in my lap. "Happy New Year," he said.

"Is this for me?"

"Sure. It's just some caramels. You like caramels?"

(Never eat caramels, Aunt Adele always said. They *ruin* the teeth.)

"Sure," I said, "I love caramels."

"Well, eat one then, for Pete's sake."

"I will." I opened the bag and unwrapped the cellophane from one of the caramels. "Did—did you buy them for me?"

"There's nobody else around, is there?" He gestured with his hand around the car.

"Thank you," I said, chewing with some difficulty. I didn't feel so sad or worried now, but more like laughing because I was driving along with Tony Jordan and he had given me a bag of candy. "They're good. Here, have one." I held out the bag and he took a caramel, wrinkling the paper between his fingers.

But my problems soon came rushing back. When we got to the path that led down to the lake, Tony stopped the car at the clearing and took another caramel, fiddling thoughtfully with the cellophane. "Hey," he said, "I was wondering if you'd like to go to a movie or something tonight?"

He was really, truly asking me for a date!

He made it sound very casual, as though he had just now thought of it and it wasn't even all that important.

And yet I knew it was important to him.

"Well?" he said, when I didn't answer at once.

"I—I don't think so, Tony." What excuse could I make?

"Listen, if it's that waitress at the cafe you're worried about, don't. Sue's a good friend of mine. She has been for a long time. You shouldn't listen to Darlene so much."

"It's not that at all," I said, thrilled that he didn't have a girlfriend. "I don't think my aunt would want me to go out on a school night, you know. I—I have lots of homework."

He looked at me silently, thinking about my answer. Then he grinned his lazy, amused grin. "Okay. How about Saturday night, then?"

Oh, if I only could!

"I'll ask my aunt," I said. But I knew I could never go out with Tony, Saturday or any other night.

"Hey"—he reached up and cuffed my chin playfully—"relax. It's only a date, not the end of the world."

I didn't stay to talk, thinking that if I got right home Aunt Frances might think I had come on the bus again. But as I ran along the Lake Road the bag of candy in my pocket felt as big and bulky as a football—and just as noticeable—and I was sure it must be written all over my face that I had been riding with Tony.

When I reached the house it was just about the same time I had gotten home the day before. I thought everything was going to work out okay, but Aunt Frances came out of the kitchen frowning.

"Hello, Lorrie," she said—rather ominously, I thought. Through the kitchen door I could see Aunt

Frances's coat draped on the back of a kitchen chair and a brown grocery bag on the table.

"I decided to do some errands in Greenwood this afternoon," Aunt Frances said, "and it was just about four-twenty when I finished, so I drove by the bus station to give you a ride home, but you weren't there."

There was nothing else I could say. "Tony Jordan drove me home."

"I see." Aunt Frances paused a moment, then continued, speaking slowly and carefully and firmly. "Lorrie, I've asked you not to come home with that boy anymore. He's not the right kind of friend for you. We've been all over this. I thought you told him yesterday that you were going to start coming home on the bus now."

"No, I didn't tell him. I didn't even see him yesterday."

Aunt Frances drew herself up very straight. "Well, Lorrie, I must say I'm disappointed in you. After all I've said, you seem to be deliberately disobeying me."

We stood staring at each other. Neither one of us knew what else to say.

Finally Aunt Frances looked away, murmuring, more to herself than to me, "Adele's probably right. Lynden Hall would be better."

I lowered my eyes without answering. I knew Aunt Frances really didn't want me to go away. That was what I was counting on.

"I'll pick you up after school myself, Lorrie," Aunt Frances decided. "That's probably the best answer. I'm only trying to do what's right."

# 14

In the winter Willow Lake was like a Christmas card picture with snow-covered trees, skaters on the ice, and the dark line of the woods rising beyond the lake houses.

I can still remember the excitement I had felt when Aunt Frances had said we were going to live there all year. I can remember the girl at school who had said, "Oh, Lorrie, how can you stand it, leaving the city and everything?"

I can remember walking around the lake with Barbara as she talked about starting college; and the special feeling of that summer, when gradually the houses had grown empty, shuttered and silent, and the Ramseys had closed their little store for the season. I can remember the bright autumn days, the first snowfall.

Willow Lake was the place I loved most in all the world. It's hard to believe that I lost it, hard to believe that

I can ever stop missing it or can ever again think of it without thinking, too, about Tony Jordan.

January and the beginning of February were cold. Icicles hung from tree branches and the edges of roofs, and the snow-banked birdbaths waited for summer on the snow-deep lawn of our house. And there were so many things still to come, I thought, like being snowbound again. Evenings spent reading in front of the fire seemed to stretch out ahead of me for weeks to come and then, one day, were suddenly gone. I was not to spend even one entire winter there, and the day I left was still and dark-skied—as if there were going to be snow; but I wasn't there to see it and never would see it snow at Willow Lake again.

But it wasn't until almost the middle of February that I left; I had begun to feel secure, sure I wouldn't ever leave. The last week in January a new semester began at Greenwood High School and I felt now I was safe. I was past the halfway point of the school year. Aunt Frances was meeting me in front of the main school entrance every afternoon at three to drive me home, and I tried to tell myself I didn't miss going to Andy's with Darlene or riding home with Tony.

I told Darlene that my aunt thought it was silly for me to wait around every day for the 4:20 bus, and I sort of hinted that Aunt Frances didn't especially approve of Andy's anyway. Darlene had always been suspicious that Aunt Frances was strict, and she wasn't all that surprised.

"Gee, Lorrie, that's too bad—maybe she'll change her mind after a while," she said, and I let it go at that.

When I started going home with Aunt Frances I won-

116

dered how many times Tony would come by the bus station looking for me, wondering where I was. He could call me up, I thought forlornly, if he really wonders where I am.

About a week after I started going home with Aunt Frances, Darlene told me at our locker between classes that Tony had been in Andy's the afternoon before.

"Was he?" I asked and I felt funny just to hear her say his name.

"Yes, he was." Darlene answered slowly, a teasing smile on her face. "I think he was looking for you."

"Looking for me?" I picked at the binding of my Spanish book. "Why should he be looking for me?"

Darlene was unwrapping a fresh stick of gum.

"Did he say he was looking for me?"

"Not exactly," she said, "but I think he was. I was with Steve, and Tony sat with us, and then when he got up to go he kind of looked around at all the other booths, and then he asked why you didn't come here anymore."

"What did you say?"

"I told him your aunt said you had to come right home after school. I told him she picks you up."

"What did he say then?"

"Nothing much. Something about how that sounded like a good setup. Then he went out."

And so the days passed, very slowly. Nothing was as much fun anymore, and I really felt left out of things not going to Andy's. Most of all I missed seeing Tony, and the only thing that made me feel good at all during those weeks was the start of the new semester and the security that seemed to mean.

Aunt Frances must have felt that everything was under control now and Tony was out of my life forever; one Friday, the end of the second week of the new semester, she asked me if I would come home on the bus that afternoon. She was going into New York for the day and wouldn't be back in time to pick me up after school.

I went to the library after my last class. But I couldn't concentrate on my work. I kept thinking how I could have gone to Andy's and Aunt Frances would never have known. I felt restless, and finally I left the library; anything was better than sitting there thinking about how good things used to be. I left the school building and walked along slowly because I had extra time before the bus. I looked across the street at Andy's, walking even slower. If someone saw me and came running out to call me in, should I go? Aunt Frances would understand if I just ran in for a minute.

No one came running out to call me in, but just as I reached the corner and turned away from Andy's I heard my name.

"Hey, Lorrie—wait up!"

It was Darlene. She had just come out of Andy's and was hurrying to catch up with me as she tied a scarf around her neck.

"Where's your aunt?"

"She couldn't come today."

"Oh." Darlene had the scarf tied and fell into step beside me. "Going to the bus?"

When I nodded she said, "I'll walk with you. I have to go to Woolworth's and get some mascara."

We hadn't seen each other very much the past few weeks, except brief moments at the locker between classes. We didn't even have the same lunch period this semester. "What's new?" Darlene asked.

"Nothing much," I replied.

"Me neither," she said. "Same old stuff."

"How's Steve?"

"Okay."

And so we walked along talking together. It was the last time we ever did. And it was my last time to walk along the Greenwood streets; remembering that afternoon, I wish I had noticed more and could keep the details of every house and shop along the way and the picture of Darlene, her black hair poking in wisps from the edge of her scarf, more clearly in my mind.

When we got to the bus stop, Darlene offered to wait a few minutes with me. A few people were sitting on the benches, so we decided to stand near the curb. Darlene did most of the talking. She had always liked to tell me her problems. Her sister Anna May was still stingy with her clothes, and her little brother had spilled orange pop on a book report she had just finished; her father didn't think she needed a new skirt for the Valentine's Day dance at school—and she really *did*, especially a certain one she had seen at the Sears store at the shopping center: it had pockets and a gold belt. I wished I could say something more than just, "Oh, that's too bad, Darlene," something that would have expressed my feeling of friendship for her and reminded her that even if I couldn't go to Andy's with her after school, she was still my best friend.

"Well," she said at last, "it's almost four-twenty." We both looked down the street, but the bus wasn't in sight.

"Wouldn't it be great if Tony came by and drove you

home," Darlene remarked cheerfully. "It's too bad he doesn't know you're here."

I started to say something, but suddenly she turned to me and nudged me. "Gee, I almost forgot to tell you. You'll never guess what I found out about Tony!"

A thousand wild thoughts flooded my mind in the fraction of a second before she went on.

"It's about that car. You know all this time he's been driving it around like he was such a big shot, and Steve told me it's really his brother's car—you know, the one who has the garage—and Tony just pretends that it's his!"

"Oh," I said faintly, so relieved I almost laughed.

"But Lorrie, don't you think that's terrible? All this time letting everybody think it was *his* car. What a show-off!"

Before I could say anything we heard a horn honking. "Oh, look," Darlene cried, "speak of the devil!"

As we looked up the street, we saw Tony coming toward us, and then I didn't feel like laughing about the car after all; I felt sad. Tony didn't really have much to call his own and it impressed everybody a lot that he had his own car. Now I knew he didn't even have that.

"Come on, Lorrie"—Darlene giggled—"let's go tease him about his car."

I caught her arm. "Oh, *no*, Darlene—"

"Why not? Come on, Lorrie. He probably wants to drive you home."

"Darlene—" I tried to keep my voice down, and I didn't let go of her arm. Tony honked again, and the people sitting on the benches were watching us now. "Please, Darlene, don't say anything about the car. That wouldn't be nice."

120

"Oh, Lorrie, don't be silly."

"Darlene, no, please. I—I won't go if you're going to say anything about the car."

Darlene hesitated, then said, "Oh, all right, all right. But I still don't see why not."

We approached the car, and Tony rolled down the window.

"Hi," Darlene began. "Are you going to drive Lorrie home?"

Tony looked at me. "I don't know," he said. "Am I going to drive you home?"

I had forgotten how handsome he really was. It seemed such a long time since I'd seen him. I *couldn't* say no and watch him drive away without me.

"All right," I said.

Just this one time won't matter, I thought. No one will ever know.

As I got into the car Darlene said good-bye, gave me a knowing smile, and hurried into Woolworth's for her mascara.

As we drove off, I let my books slide down onto the seat between us, the way they always had. I thought seeing them there might remind him to tease me about them, but he didn't seem to notice.

"So where have you been?" he asked rather roughly.

"Oh . . . around."

He didn't say anything more for a long time, and I wondered how he had happened to come by the bus stop after Darlene had already told him I was now going home with Aunt Frances.

At last, almost as though he'd read my thoughts, he said, "I was kind of surprised to see you. I heard you get picked up right at school now.''

"That's right." I tried to keep my voice steady. "You see, my aunt just thought it would be easier for me—and she's in town a lot in the afternoons doing errands, so she just picks me up.''

It sounded like a big hodgepodge of lies to me, and I couldn't even look at Tony.

"I thought you just didn't want to ride home with me anymore," he said.

"Oh, *no*, it's nothing like that at all.''

"I don't know." He didn't sound convinced. "I kind of get the idea that your aunt doesn't want you hanging around with me, seeing as I'm such a bum.''

"Tony!" I jerked my head around to look at him. "You're not a bum!''

I must have amused him with my exclamation. He relaxed a little and began to laugh. "Okay, so I'm not a bum." Then after a moment he continued more seriously. "But you know what I mean—like these books. Look at the books!" He motioned at the books on the seat between us. "You know so much, kiddo," he said. "All the stuff that's in those books. And me . . .'' He shrugged and left the sentence unfinished.

I thought for a moment he was going to say that he didn't even own the car he pretended was his, but he didn't. He began to speak more brightly. "Oh, well, I got this car and money in my pocket. I guess things could be worse.''

I was glad he didn't know I knew about the car. I was willing to go on pretending it was his, if he wanted me to think it was.

"Hey," he said, "remember the time we came out here?"

I looked out of the window. We were just passing the hill where we had watched Darlene and Steve sledding. "You mean when we were with Darlene and Steve?" I asked.

"Yeah. That was fun."

"But we only watched."

"But it was fun, wasn't it? Didn't you have fun that day?"

"Sure," I said. "I had fun."

When we reached the road to the lake, he pulled to the side of the highway. He took my hand and sat looking at me.

"You know what, kiddo?"

"What?"

"I was just thinking . . . we never did have much fun together, did we?"

"What do you mean?"

"Ah, you know. I was always teasing you—you know. But I never meant it. I think you're a real sweet girl."

Afterward, when I realized that it was the last day for so many things—going to Greenwood High School, walking with Darlene, waiting at the bus station—I always thought about what Tony said, and it was almost as if he'd had a premonition that it was the last time we would ever sit in the car by the edge of the path that led down to the lake, talking in the gathering dusk of a winter afternoon.

"What about that Saturday night?" he asked, after what seemed an eternity. "Did you ever ask your aunt?"

I couldn't think of anything to say and sat forlornly

staring down at our clasped hands. Finally I heard myself saying, "She thinks I'm too young to date."

We both saw the car at the same time, a dark blue Olds approaching from the opposite direction. It was Aunt Frances returning from the city. She saw us, of course, as she slowed to make the turn to the side road that led down to the lake; she almost stopped—but then she went on.

I had forgotten Aunt Frances even existed!

"There's your aunt," Tony said casually.

Everything was going wrong! What was I going to do now?

"I better go." I began to gather up my books with a sense of panic.

"Lorrie," Tony said softly, "ask her again. That is, if you want to go out with me."

"Sure I do, Tony." I fumbled with the door handle, my face turned away from him, my heart already beginning to pound with fear at what was ahead for me.

"Hey," Tony called as I opened the door and got out, "you forgot one." He was holding out a book to me. "Be careful," he teased. "You go leaving your books around like that and I might read one."

But his teasing didn't sound quite the same. Maybe I could have gotten him interested in school again.

When I didn't reach back to take the book, he leaned across the seat and added it to the stack I had in my arms. "Here," he said. Then he reached out and softly touched my cheek.

"See you, kiddo," he said as I turned and began to run across the snowy ground to the path down to the lake.

## 15

Late that February, after I had left, there was a terrible storm in the area around Willow Lake. It was reported in the newspapers, and I read all about it one morning sitting in the dining room at Lynden Hall. "Say, Lorrie," one of the girls asked me, "isn't that where you live, around there?"

"Yes," I said, "that's where I live."

The paper reported:

A savage snowstorm and heavy winds battered a section of northern New Jersey this weekend. Hardest hit, and still enduring subfreezing temperatures, is the area around Dartham, with lake areas and neighboring small towns also suffering. More than eighteen inches of snow has fallen in most sections, and there are a few reports of depths to twenty-four inches in others.

Under the lashing of the wind-driven storm all transportation and business is at a standstill. Schools have closed in Dartham, Greenwood, Lowville, and Clarendon. The airport in Lowville has canceled all flights, and weekend vacationers at lake lodges are virtually stranded, with more snow in sight.

Power lines are down in many sections, and damages reported in the wake of the storm are already extensive.

This is the most severe storm to hit that section of the state in twenty years.

I called Aunt Frances and to my surprise got through to her right away. She assured me that she was all right—not even any falling trees on the porch this time. The electricity was off, but she was sure it would soon be on again.

I went up to my room, but I couldn't keep my mind on studying. I felt so far away from everything. And so terribly alone. On my desk a small framed photograph of Barbara reminded me of other, happier days.

My roommate at Lynden Hall was a girl named Sara Abbott, a sweet-natured, blue-eyed girl with yellow hair as fine as corn silk. She felt sorry for me and asked me a lot about Willow Lake and how I happened to come to Lynden Hall after the semester had started. I never said much to her about Willow Lake; she didn't seem like the type of girl who would have cared about it particularly. But she was nice to me, and she often said she wished I wouldn't look so sad.

"Didn't you *want* to come here?" she asked me with surprise one day.

And I said, "No, I liked living at Willow Lake."

Another time, a Saturday afternoon, we were studying and it began to snow outside. I said I supposed Mr. Ramsey had built a fire for the ice skaters.

"Don't feel so bad," Sara said. "It's only one winter, Lorrie. You'll have lots of other winters to be there, if you like it so much."

Sara was friendly. All the girls at Lynden Hall were friendly. But I continued to think of Darlene as my best friend and none of the girls at Lynden Hall was able to take her place. I missed her, with her black hair and eye makeup and chocolate-covered raisins.

I had seen Darlene for a few minutes the day I went with Aunt Frances to transfer from Greenwood High School. Aunt Frances and I were waiting in the office, and I had seen Darlene going by in the hallway. I told Aunt Frances I would be right back, and I went out to the hall to tell Darlene I was going to Lynden Hall.

"Lorrie!" she exclaimed with astonishment. "Oh, Lorrie, no! You can't!" She could hardly believe that I could be leaving so suddenly. And it's hard to say good-bye to your best friend in only a minute or two, with the bell already ringing for the next class.

"Oh, Lorrie," Darlene wailed. "I've got to go, but I just can't believe it! What will I do!" She started away slowly, then turned back. "I'll see you in the summer, Lorrie. Call me as soon as you get back."

"I will," I promised. The bell was ringing and I knew that Darlene would be late for her class. She disappeared with a few other stragglers hurrying down the hall. I hadn't even had time to ask her to say good-bye to Tony for me.

As I went back into the office I still couldn't believe that

I was really transferring. Surely *something* would happen to save me at the last moment. The air seemed to vibrate with the feeling of crisis, as in a book.

But nothing happened.

As the days passed at Lynden Hall, I began to look forward to the Easter holiday in April. But about the middle of March Aunt Frances telephoned me and said that I had been invited to Aunt Adele's for Easter, and she thought it would be best if I went.

"Are you coming?" I asked.

"Well, dear . . ." She seemed to hesitate. "I thought maybe I wouldn't. I'm very busy just now." She paused. "But Barbara will be home, and I know you'll have a good time. Aunt Adele wants you to come very much."

I bought a bottle of Chanel cologne to take to Aunt Adele, and I told her everything was okay at school.

"Oh, Lorrie, I'm so happy that you like it," she said, hugging me like she used to when I was a little girl. "I'm so happy," she repeated. "I always knew you'd like Lynden Hall. It's really where you belong, dear. Everything is just working out splendidly, isn't it?"

The cologne surprised her. "Lorrie—you remembered I like Chanel. How sweet of you."

I was a sweet girl—Tony had said so. I wondered what he was doing now, if he missed me, if he was waiting for summer vacation as eagerly as I was.

Aunt Adele stood looking out of the living room windows at the city, daubing a drop of Chanel behind her ear. "Isn't New York beautiful in the spring?" she said. She didn't really understand that I was thinking about something else entirely.

She had organized some activities for Barbara and me; and of course Eric Anders was around a lot of the time, as he had been at Christmas.

Nobody talked about Willow Lake, however, until one night when Barbara came into the guest room, which had been given to me because Aunt Frances wasn't there. I was ready for bed, sitting propped up against the pillows looking at one of Aunt Adele's glossy fashion magazines.

"Lorrie?" Barbara had sort of a conspiratorial note in her voice. "Can I talk to you for a minute?"

"Sure." I moved over so she could sit on the edge of the bed. "Why are you whispering?"

She held a finger to her lips, and I heard a murmur of voices down the hall and then the closing of a door.

"Mother and Daddy are going out," Barbara explained. "But I heard Mother telling Daddy something today, and I just *had* to tell you."

"What was it?"

Barbara continued to talk softly, although we were alone in the apartment now. "Mother told Daddy that Aunt Frances told her that the other day she was in her studio painting, and she happened to look up out of her window and there was this boy standing on the Lake Road looking at the house. She said he didn't see her, and she watched him for a long time."

"What was he doing?"

"Nothing." Barbara shivered with excitement. "That was it! He wasn't doing *anything*. He was just standing there, looking at the house, and then after a long time he walked away."

I waited, and Barbara wriggled impatiently. "Don't

129

you understand, Lorrie? Don't you know who it was?''

"I—I'm not sure," I answered. My fingers felt cold and I twisted them together to stop their trembling. The magazine slid down across the covers.

"I think it's the most intriguing thing." Barbara's face was bright with excitement. She smoothed back her hair and then clasped her hands under her chin. "Mother told Daddy that Aunt Frances said it was that boy who used to drive you home from school." She looked at me expectantly.

"I told you about him," I said. "You remember."

"I remember," she said. "His name was . . . ?"

"Tony Jordan." It was hard to say his name. It made me want to cry.

"Oh, Lorrie." Barbara sighed. "It sounds so romantic. I always wondered why you suddenly started going to Lynden Hall right in the middle of the year. I always thought there was *something*. But Mother always said it was none of my business. What happened, Lorrie? You can tell me."

I shook my head. "Nothing exactly *happened*. Aunt Frances just didn't like it because he quit school. She didn't want me to ride home with him. But I did, and . . . and then she said I had to go to Lynden Hall."

Barbara looked at me sympathetically. "Lorrie—how awful for you. You really liked him a lot?"

"I liked him a lot."

She was waiting for me to say more.

"He's very handsome." I could hear tears in my voice. "And he—he has a car of his own."

"That's wonderful," Barbara said. "Oh, he must be in

130

love with you to come around after you'd gone and stand looking at the house. I think it's *so* romantic.''

"I never had a real date with him." My voice was low. It was hard to talk about it, even to Barbara. "He wanted to take me to the movies once, but I went to Lynden Hall instead.''

It was a poor joke. Even Barbara didn't laugh.

She got up reluctantly, patting my hand. "I just thought you'd like to know—about him coming to the lake house.'' At the doorway she turned around and looked back at me thoughtfully. "There was something else that Mother said. . . .'' She hesitated, as if not quite sure whether to tell me what it was.

"Well, Mother told Daddy that she's afraid if you go back there this summer, what's-his-name—Tony—will turn up again.''

But that was what I was hoping for. I was counting the days till summer came!

I lay awake a long time that night, thinking about what Barbara had said. Her words echoed in my mind: If you go back there this summer, Tony will turn up again. *If* you go back . . . *If* you go back . . . But there wasn't any other place to go!

I was wrong about that. I had been back at school only a few days when Aunt Frances wrote me a long letter explaining that she had sold the house at Willow Lake. My hands shook, and before I was halfway through the letter my eyes were so full of tears I couldn't even read any-more. I remembered Darlene's last hurried words: "I'll see you in the summer, Lorrie.'' And I remembered my roommate Sara saying, "It's only one winter, Lorrie.

You'll have lots of other winters to be there, if you like it so much.'' And they were both wrong.

Aunt Frances wrote:

I hope you won't feel too badly, dear. I've been doing a lot of thinking since you left. [I could picture her kind face creased by lines of doubt and worry.] And it really seemed the wisest thing to do, considering everything. It isn't the same for me here alone as when you were here. I thought if you're away at school now and then later you'll be away at college, I might as well be in New York, as Adele says. And it's time we started traveling some during the summers, seeing some of the country. We've hardly seen anything, and doesn't that seem a shame?

I thought, for instance, this summer we might go out west somewhere. There are some spots in southwest Texas that haven't been done much, at least not by painters exhibiting in New York. I might do some portraits of Indian children. That's just one idea. There are so many places we've never seen.

A very lovely family has bought the lake house. They were interested in it for a long time now, and that was one of the reasons I felt too busy to get to Adele's at Easter; and I've postponed the exhibit I was going to have this spring. Next fall will be time enough. I was lucky to find a buyer; real estate is moving so slowly these days. There are so many details to attend to in matters like this, and oh, the packing! Mrs. Peck comes out extra days to help—and I'll leave some of it for the movers to do. I'll stay with Adele until our new apartment is settled. By the time school is out this June I expect to have everything done, and we'll be all set to travel.

I cried a lot over Aunt Frances's letter. I felt betrayed, and I understood why she'd wanted me to go to Aunt Adele's at Easter. She hadn't wanted me to know she was trying to sell the house. And now I knew that she expected me to be attending Lynden Hall next year, too. Then I would graduate and go away to college. I would never see Tony Jordan again.

Aunt Frances waited a few days—giving me a chance to get used to all the things in her letter—and then she phoned me at school one day. I couldn't think of anything to say, and I was afraid if I tried to say what I felt I'd start to cry.

"It's all for the best, dear." Aunt Frances's voice was as clear as if she were standing beside me instead of phoning from miles away. "And you mustn't ever feel that your Aunt Adele persuaded me against my own wishes, about sending you to Lynden Hall or selling the house. I see myself that it *is* the best plan, for everyone."

It wasn't the best plan for me! It was an awful plan! I wished I was dead!

"And, Lorrie . . ." There was hesitation in Aunt Frances's voice. After a slight pause she went on. "You remember that boy Barbara was so fond of when she was in high school last year?"

I didn't say anything. I was still fighting tears and a lump in my throat.

"Don't you see?" Aunt Frances was trying to sound cheerful and comforting. "Barbara was so upset at the time, and now she's met Eric and she's happier than she ever was with that other boy."

I knew what Aunt Frances was trying to do. She was telling me there would be other boys for me. "You'll have lots of boyfriends someday," Darlene had said. Right now I didn't want anybody but Tony.

I knew Aunt Frances was trying to make me feel better, and there wasn't anything more to say after that. I mumbled, "Bye," and hung up.

Sometimes, lying awake at night, I wondered if we were all somehow miraculously given the chance to go back and do things over, would we do anything differently? And I knew that I wouldn't. As grief-stricken as I was to think of what had been done, I knew I would do the same thing again if I were given a thousand chances. I would never have hurt Darlene's feelings and I could never have been really happy at Willow Lake without seeing Tony. It wouldn't have been the same, after all, to stay there and not be with them.

At last the spring term was over. I took the train into New York with several other girls from school, and as I got off I could see Aunt Frances waving to me. As she came toward me I saw tears in her eyes, and I realized that she, too, had lost Willow Lake, and she had loved it as much as I loved it. She had sounded so matter-of-fact over the telephone, I hadn't thought she might be as sad as I was.

But there was no going back, and I ran to meet her. She hugged me and kissed me and said she was crying because she was so happy to see me. Then, when we had put my suitcases into the trunk of the car and were weaving through the traffic in the familiar, noisy, steaming New York City streets, Aunt Frances began telling me all about our new apartment—making it sound as if there was nothing so nice as a city apartment after all—and about all the plans she had made for us and all the interesting things we were going to do that summer.

Staring out of the car window I imagined I saw Willow Lake for a moment, warm and green, and the children splashing around the pier.

I tried to listen to Aunt Frances. She said the summer ahead was going to be exciting and full of fun, and I knew whatever it was it would be different, different from all the summers I could remember. I had been such a little girl when she'd bought the lake house, and I couldn't remember any summers but those spent at Willow Lake.

I knew someday there would be other places I could love, and other people; but I also knew I would never forget a place called Willow Lake, and a boy named Tony Jordan.

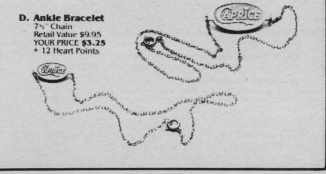